Saved by the Shotgun

"Custis, we're trapped! They'll kill us for sure."

"Not if I kill them first."

Longarm's eyes were finally beginning to adjust to the bad light. He suddenly made out the d___ ___ ___ ___ lie's shotgun. Snatchi__ ___ ___ ___ ple of shells for the s___

"They're . . . they'__ ___ ___ ___ pered, voice fading.

Longarm found the ___ ___ ___ reloaded the shotgun. ___ ___ ___ quiet," he ordered, spotting a ladder ___ding up to the loft as the barn doors began to open inch by inch.

Longarm sprinted to the ladder and went up it fast. He dropped on his stomach in grass hay and shoved the shotgun into the open air just as the barn doors burst open.

The four Dooley men were bold and stupid with rage and bloodlust. For just a fraction of a second they were silhouetted against the bright light of day, and that was when Longarm pulled both barrels down and delivered a murderous volley of thunder from on high . . .

DON'T MISS THESE
ALL-ACTION WESTERN SERIES
FROM THE BERKLEY PUBLISHING GROUP

THE GUNSMITH by J. R. Roberts
Clint Adams was a legend among lawmen, outlaws, and ladies. They called him . . . the Gunsmith.

LONGARM by Tabor Evans
The popular long-running series about Deputy U.S. Marshal Custis Long—his life, his loves, his fight for justice.

SLOCUM by Jake Logan
Today's longest-running action Western. John Slocum rides a deadly trail of hot blood and cold steel.

BUSHWHACKERS by B. J. Lanagan
An action-packed series by the creators of Longarm! The rousing adventures of the most brutal gang of cutthroats ever assembled—Quantrill's Raiders.

DIAMONDBACK by Guy Brewer
Dex Yancey is Diamondback, a Southern gentleman turned con man when his brother cheats him out of the family fortune. Ladies love him. Gamblers hate him. But nobody pulls one over on Dex . . .

WILDGUN by Jack Hanson
The blazing adventures of mountain man Will Barlow—from the creators of Longarm!

TEXAS TRACKER by Tom Calhoun
J.T. Law: the most relentless—and dangerous—manhunter in all Texas. Where sheriffs and posses fail, he's the best man to bring in the most vicious outlaws—for a price.

TABOR EVANS

LONGARM

AND THE VANISHING LADY

JOVE BOOKS, NEW YORK

THE BERKLEY PUBLISHING GROUP
Published by the Penguin Group
Penguin Group (USA) Inc.
375 Hudson Street, New York, New York 10014, USA
Penguin Group (Canada), 90 Eglinton Avenue East, Suite 700, Toronto, Ontario M4P 2Y3, Canada
(a division of Pearson Penguin Canada Inc.) • Penguin Books Ltd., 80 Strand, London WC2R 0RL,
England • Penguin Group Ireland, 25 St. Stephen's Green, Dublin 2, Ireland (a division of Penguin
Books Ltd.) • Penguin Group (Australia), 250 Camberwell Road, Camberwell, Victoria 3124, Australia
(a division of Pearson Australia Group Pty. Ltd.) • Penguin Books India Pvt. Ltd., 11 Community
Centre, Panchsheel Park, New Delhi—110 017, India • Penguin Group (NZ), 67 Apollo Drive,
Rosedale, Auckland 0632, New Zealand (a division of Pearson New Zealand Ltd.) • Penguin Books
(South Africa) (Pty.) Ltd., 24 Sturdee Avenue, Rosebank, Johannesburg 2196, South Africa

Penguin Books Ltd., Registered Offices: 80 Strand, London WC2R 0RL, England

This is a work of fiction. Names, characters, places, and incidents either are the product of the author's
imagination or are used fictitiously, and any resemblance to actual persons, living or dead, business
establishments, events, or locales is entirely coincidental.

LONGARM AND THE VANISHING LADY

A Jove Book / published by arrangement with the author

PUBLISHING HISTORY
Jove edition / October 2012

ISBN: 978-0-515-15112-1

JOVE®
Jove Books are published by The Berkley Publishing Group,
a division of Penguin Group (USA) Inc.,
375 Hudson Street, New York, New York 10014.
JOVE® is a registered trademark of Penguin Group (USA) Inc.
The "J" design is a trademark of Penguin Group (USA) Inc.

PRINTED IN THE UNITED STATES OF AMERICA

10 9 8 7 6 5 4 3 2 1

ALWAYS LEARNING   **PEARSON**

Chapter 1

Deputy United States Marshal Custis Long was enjoying a splendid Sunday afternoon in downtown Denver when a carriage careened wildly around the corner of Colfax Avenue and nearly ran him over as he was crossing the street. In the fraction of a second before he had to dive into a horse trough in order to save himself, Longarm saw that the carriage was a runaway and that an older man was lying slumped across the lap of a terrified and quite beautiful young woman. Longarm scrambled out of the horse trough with water cascading off his clothes. He ran to the nearest hitching post, untied a tall buckskin and threw himself into the saddle. He wasn't a cowboy, but Longarm was no slouch when it came to riding fast horses, and he soon had the buckskin racing down Colfax after the carriage.

As he drew abreast of a fine pair of sorrels that were running wild-eyed and terrified through Denver's downtown, he glanced at the woman, who seemed to be frozen in fear. Longarm saw that the reins had been dropped and that there was little the woman could do but pray and hope that the carriage did not roll and crush her to death.

"Hang on!" he shouted, urging his horse past the carriage in the hope of being able to grab the bit of one of the horses and drag it to a standstill.

But just as he was about to reach out and try to take control, the carriage whipped back and forth before slamming sideways against a heavy freight wagon, which caused the back wheels to disintegrate. The carriage's axle made a terrible shriek as it skidded across cobblestones and then smashed into a hitching post, tossing the young woman through the air. Longarm barely escaped being hit by the out-of-control carriage, which then struck an elm tree and was torn almost in half. Miraculously, the matched pair of runaway horses continued racing down Colfax dragging only a few pieces of splintered wood.

Longarm managed to rein the buckskin to a sliding stop and then he threw himself out of the saddle and hit the ground running.

When he reached the young woman she was semi-conscious and bleeding from a number of scrapes, but there did not appear to be any heavy loss of blood. The older man that had been with her in the carriage was lying halfway under the sidewalk like a broken, discarded rag doll. Two men were already at his side trying to revive him, but Longarm had a feeling the older man had been dead even before the crash.

"Miss!" Longarm shouted, making a quick assessment of her condition.

Her most serious bleeding seemed to come from the chest area, and Longarm hoped that she had not had her rib cage crushed and her lungs fatally punctured. He tore open her bodice and saw that she had been impaled in her right breast by a thick sliver of wood. Longarm pulled it out and used his clean handkerchief to staunch the flow as he cradled her head in his lap. "Miss, can you hear me?"

The young woman shook herself and her blue eyes focused on Longarm's anxious face for a moment before she struggled to get to her feet. "What . . ."

"You've been in an awful accident. Don't move yet. Just try and relax and stay still until we can get a doctor to look you over."

The young woman looked down at her chest and her eyes widened with fear and then embarrassment. She pushed his hand off her large right breast and the blood immediately welled out of the splinter hole. The wound must have hurt very much, and she clamped her own hand back over it and his now blood-soaked handkerchief.

"My father . . . is he . . . dead?" she whispered.

Longarm glanced back over his shoulder and saw the two men rise up from the body and shake their heads. He turned to the anxious young woman. "I'm afraid that he is."

A sob escaped her lips and tears rolled down her cheeks. "Father had a very bad heart. It had failed him several times these past few years and I was able to help him, but this time . . . everything went terribly wrong."

"I'm sorry, but it was your father's time . . . not yours."

She looked down at her bare chest and lifted the handkerchief for a moment. "Then I'm *not* dying?"

"No," he said, holding up the splinter. "Look. This is the bloody splinter that I removed from your breast. It was thick but not very long and it came out cleanly. I'm sure that as soon as a doctor gets here they'll take you to a hospital and you'll do just fine."

"Thank you," she whispered, trying to pull up the top of her dress in a gesture of modesty. "I saw you try to grab the horse's bit and attempt to drag him to a stop. But when our carriage struck something . . . well . . . I can't remember anything after that moment."

"Do you have pain inside your head . . . or in your spine?"

She touched her head, then shifted her weight just a bit. "No. I don't think so. But I'm not feeling very well and I'm devastated to learn that I've lost my father."

"How old was he?" Longarm asked, just trying to make conversation until a doctor was summoned and could get to their side.

"My father was sixty-eight."

"And your mother?"

"She died many years ago."

"A husband . . . children that need to know . . ."

"My husband was accidentally shot in Cheyenne last winter and we didn't have time to have any children."

"I'm sorry to hear that," Longarm said. "What about any brothers or sisters that live here in Denver that we can get in touch with?"

"I'm an only child. My father is all that I have . . . or had." She shook her head and bit her lower lip to keep from sobbing. "Father and I only came to Denver this spring. He bought a downtown hotel and I helped him manage it. We were both starting over fresh but because of his failing heart he knew he was living on borrowed time."

"Don't you have anyone here that needs to know what happened?"

"I've an uncle," she said. "His name is John Holt and he owns . . ."

"The Frontier Hotel," Longarm said. "I know and like Mr. Holt. He was once the mayor of Denver."

"Yes. And that's where we're staying. But John is now in his mid-eighties and I don't want to give him a fright. He also has heart trouble and this news might kill him." The woman grabbed Longarm and in a pleading voice, she said, "Don't tell him what happened this morning! I'll do that, but I'll need a little time first."

"Of course. What is your name?"

"Lillian . . . but everyone calls me Lilly. Lilly St. Clair."

"My name is Custis Long. I'm a United States deputy marshal and I work at the Federal Building just up the street."

"You're very brave to have tried to reach out and stop my horses."

"I probably would have fallen out of the saddle and gotten run over by the carriage if it hadn't struck something and flipped," he said with a smile.

"I don't believe that," she told him.

Just then a doctor in his fifties with a well-worn medical kit arrived. "Move aside," he ordered brusquely, almost knocking Longarm over with his whiskey-reeking breath. "I need to examine this young woman!"

The moment Longarm moved aside, the doctor tore Lilly's dress down to her waist, exposing both of her breasts to the gathering crowd so that the men among them leered, openmouthed.

"Doctor," Longarm said, angered by the man's insensitivity, "I pulled a splinter from her right breast and it wasn't in deep. You don't have to do this right out here in the street."

"Don't tell me what I do need to do or not do!"

Longarm had seen a lot of fine doctors in his time and a few had even saved his life. He'd also had to suffer the incompetence of plenty of "tooth pullers" and quacks that had little or no formal medical training. And most important, Longarm could immediately spot a competent and professional doctor from a bad one.

He reached down, grabbed the quack by the collar, and shoved him away. "I'll take Miss St. Clair straight to the hospital," he announced loud enough to be heard by everyone. "And all the rest of you folks, go on about your business. You've had your eyeful and now you need to get moving!"

"So who the hell are you to tell a *doctor* to stay away from that young woman!" a big man demanded.

Longarm reached into his vest pocket and showed everyone his federal officer's badge. "I'm taking charge here and I'm telling you all to leave right now."

The crowd that had gathered numbered at least two dozen. They slowly dispersed, most of them walking quickly over to stare at Lilly's dead father. Longarm shook his head in pure disgust. Some people were just morbid, he guessed.

"Can I try to stand?" Lilly whispered.

"If you don't think that it will hurt you, then give it a try. I'll help."

Longarm wrapped a powerful arm around Lilly and eased her to her feet. For a moment, she almost fell and then she gathered herself and took a faltering step, holding the top of her dress closed with one hand. "I want to go to my father's side," she said.

Longarm understood completely. He led her some twenty feet to ease her down at her father's side.

"I wish he could know that I wasn't hurt too badly in the crash," Lilly said, trying to hold back tears. "Father was driving when his heart suddenly failed and would have blamed himself for what happened to us next."

"I'm sure that he knows that you are going to be just fine," Longarm offered, because he couldn't think of anything more comforting to tell the grieving woman.

Lilly knelt and gently touched her father's cheek. "He had a bad heart all of his life . . . but that didn't stop him from being a great man. He built a fortune buying properties with no help from anyone. He was also the most decent and finest man I ever knew."

Longarm felt a deep sense of sadness wishing he could have said the same thing about his own late father, who now lay buried in the dark, loamy soil of West Virginia. "My father died when I was young. I wish I'd have known him as long as you knew your father."

Lilly nodded. "Father wanted to show me the West. He had been out here several times and loved it. He believed that it was the future . . . but now there is no future for him."

"Would you like me to help you?" Longarm asked.

"Yes, please."

Longarm quickly gave instructions that Lilly's father be taken to the finest funeral parlor in town adding, "Tell them that this man is to be given the best that they have to offer and that his daughter will be getting in touch with them for the details of the funeral."

The men nodded.

"Now," Longarm said, "we need you to go see a doctor."

"I'm not sure that is necessary," Lilly replied. "I'm feeling better and nothing seems to be broken."

"All the same," Longarm persisted, "it would be a very good idea."

"Will you come with me?"

"Of course."

Lilly smiled gratefully. "I've ruined your Sunday plans and I'm sorry."

"Don't give it a thought," he told her. "I really didn't have any plans for today. I was just going to get some exercise, relax, and enjoy this fine weather we are having."

She managed a smile. "You're a gentleman."

"Sometimes," he said, giving her a wink.

Lilly, despite her pain and the sorrow she was feeling for the loss of her father, squeezed his hand and said, "Unless you are married, after I get checked over at the hospital, let's find a place to eat and talk."

He brushed some debris out of her ash-blond hair and then straightened her collar. "You're a trooper."

"And that's a compliment?"

"Oh, yes. Very much so."

Lilly took his arm and Longarm walked her slowly up Colfax Avenue toward the nearest hospital. She limped and was badly banged up and scraped in many places, but she held her head high and possessed the air of a true lady. Longarm was impressed and his own chin lifted as he escorted her down the cobblestone street.

"Do you live nearby?" she asked.

"Not far."

"I live at my uncle's Frontier Hotel. My father and I took the top rooms, which are large and give us a fine view of this bustling city."

"I'll bet that the view is impressive. Denver is growing faster than weeds in the spring."

"My father and I were looking to buy more properties," Lilly explained. "We think that Denver has a very bright future."

"I'd agree with that."

"And what is in *your* future, Marshal Custis Long?"

He shrugged his broad shoulders. "I kind of like to take each day as it comes, Lilly. It's been my experience that, if you put too much thought into what you want to happen . . . it usually doesn't."

"Oh, really?"

"That's just the way I think."

"You sound like a man who lives for the day."

"I do."

"And I've ruined this one for you," she said sadly.

"Lilly, I wouldn't trade places with anyone in Denver today."

She looked up at him with surprise and tears in her blue eyes. "That's about the nicest thing I've ever heard from a man I didn't know at all well."

"Well," he told her. "Once you're feeling better, we can change that."

"My knowing you well?"

"Yes."

"Thank you, but I'm going to need a little time to mourn the passing of my father. He knew that he could die at any moment and over a year ago the doctors told him that he should get his business in order . . . which he did. Father left everything to me and I'm going to try and use my inheritance well."

"You mean to make more money."

"That, of course, but also to help others less fortunate than myself. There are so many poor people living in the cities. So many children that are hungry and barely clothed."

Longarm nodded with agreement. "There are hundreds just right here in Denver, Lilly." He gave her a wry smile. "Are you intending to become Denver's patron saint?"

"Why not?" she asked. "Less than thirty minutes ago I could have easily died in that wreck. Maybe I was put here for a good purpose."

"Maybe you were at that," he said.

"And your purpose is?"

"To be the best federal lawman I can be and just to live every day as if it were my last."

Lilly suddenly decided to change the subject. She smoothed her hair and touched a scrape on her cheekbone. "I must look like a real fright."

"Not really. Even mussed up you're one of the most beautiful women in Denver."

"You *are* a gentleman!" she said.

"When I'm with a lady I always aim to please."

Their eyes met and the corner of Lilly's mouth turned upward in a smile. "Yes, I can easily believe that."

Longarm started to say more, but being as Lilly St. Clair thought him a *complete* gentleman, he chose to hold his silence.

Chapter 2

Longarm and Lilly St. Clair left the hospital an hour later after a real doctor had examined Lilly's injuries and given her some medication for pain.

"I'm sure you want to go back to your hotel now," Longarm said.

"I'd rather go directly to the funeral parlor," she offered quietly.

"I understand. The closest and best mortuary in Denver is just up the street two blocks. Are you up to the walk?"

"Of course."

Their stop at the funeral parlor was brief. Longarm sat in a somber waiting room while Lilly made the arrangements. When she reappeared, she looked even more pale and shaken than she had when they arrived. "Custis, I think you'd better hail us a horse and buggy. I'm feeling weak and dizzy."

"I'll do that right now."

Longarm didn't have to wait long and soon he and Lilly were being delivered to the Frontier Hotel. Longarm paid the driver and helped Lilly out of the buggy, then up onto the boardwalk, saying, "You're not feeling very well at all, are you?"

"No, I'm not. But once I have a chance to lie down and rest for a while, I'm sure that I'll feel much better."

"No doubt about that," Longarm said, wanting to offer the distraught woman encouragement. He opened the hotel's front door and gave her a smile. "Here we are."

"Thank you so much for everything."

"You're more than welcome. Would you like me to help . . ."

"No, thanks. I can manage from here. The staff will be extremely upset by the death of my father and by my battered appearance. I'll want to speak to them privately."

"You've had a terrible shock and I fully I understand," Longarm said, realizing that she did not want him to accompany her into the hotel. "And if I can be of any further service, you can find me at the Marshal's Office in the Federal Building."

"I will." She touched his face and then gave him a quick hug before disappearing into the Frontier Hotel.

On Monday, Longarm stuck around the office more than usual in hopes that Lilly might appear, but she did not. He could not get the beautiful young woman out of his mind and found it hard to converse with his fellow law officers and the office staff. He'd always hated sitting behind a desk and doing paperwork and carrying on trivial conversations.

"You seem especially restless today," his boss, Billy Vail, remarked. "Anything wrong?"

"No."

"Did you have an enjoyable weekend off?"

"No."

Billy was a kind, balding man who had once been a field officer but who had been promoted to management. He and Longarm understood each other and got along very well.

"Billy?"

"Yeah?"

"When am I going to get sent out of this office? I've been hanging around here for almost a week and I'm starting to go stir-crazy."

"You want a case to work on somewhere out of Denver. Right?"

Longarm had to smile. "You know I like to be on the move and I can't sit still."

"I may have something for you," Billy mused as he sorted through his mounds of paperwork.

"And that would be?"

Billy Vail found the telegram that he'd been searching for and reached for his spectacles. "A few days ago I received this telling me that a federal officer up in Cheyenne is missing."

"For how long?"

Billy frowned. "Couple of weeks. Apparently there was a train holdup in the Laramie Mountains and this officer left to investigate and never returned."

"Maybe he's still chasing the robbers."

"Maybe," Billy agreed. "But the local marshal of Cheyenne says that no one has seen or heard of the missing lawman, who had promised to keep in contact in case he needed help."

"Well, you know how it goes sometimes, Billy. You were in the field for over ten years and well remember that there are often times when you have to cut across country on a manhunt and ride hundreds of miles from the nearest telegraph line. Makes sense to me that the train robbers would avoid towns and people for a while."

"That's true. But the Cheyenne marshal says that this fella was not one to just drop out of sight and leave people wondering about whether he was still alive or dead. He hadn't been on the job all that long, either."

"Was he married with children?"

Billy turned his attention back to the lengthy telegram and scowled. "Yep, it says he has a wife."

Longarm didn't need a lot of reasons to take a quick trip north. "I could jump on a train tomorrow and be up in Cheyenne by evening. Poke around a little and send you a telegram tomorrow."

"Let's give it one more day," Billy decided. "I only met this missing federal officer once and I have to say that he seemed plenty tough and capable even if he wasn't long on experience."

"Whatever you decide," Longarm answered. "But I sure wouldn't mind getting out of here for a couple of days. That train ride up to Cheyenne on the Denver Pacific Railroad is scenic and relaxing, and I've got plenty of good friends living up there."

"*Women* friends, I'll bet."

Longarm chuckled. "There are some beautiful women in Cheyenne but none finer than what we have right here in Denver."

Billy pushed his spectacles up on his forehead as he considered the telegram and circumstances. "Tell you what, Custis, come in by eight o'clock tomorrow morning and I'll have a telegraph ready for you to send up to Cheyenne. And, if they still haven't heard from that missing federal marshal, I think you'd better be prepared to get on the train and head on up the tracks."

"The man is probably still hunting the train robbers somewhere up in Wyoming Territory or maybe he's clear over on the western slope of the Rockies. Probably let his horse get loose and is walking back to Cheyenne embarrassed by his carelessness."

"I hope that is the case," Billy said, looking as if he doubted it. "But either way, we need to find out what happened to him and why he hasn't reported back to Cheyenne."

"I'm leaving here right now," Longarm said, "because eight o'clock is far too early to face you and this office at that hour of the morning."

"Thanks for the compliment," Billy said drily.

"No offense, Boss."

"None taken if you show up on time tomorrow morning," Billy said. "Now get out of here because you're making all of us nervous."

"I'm on my way."

Longarm had decided to stop by the Frontier Hotel and inquire as to how Lilly St. Clair was feeling but decided at the last minute to give her an extra day or two to heal and regain her composure. So he walked directly to his apartment, fed the stray alley cat that had adopted him, and took a bath. He changed his shirt, shaved, and headed out to eat and maybe have a few beers. After that, if necessary, he'd turn in early and be ready to pack a satchel and head up to Cheyenne.

His current favorite restaurant was the Sizzling Pig, which specialized in pork roast and chops drenched in a sauce that made them one of his favorite dishes. When he arrived at the Sizzling Pig before the dinner rush hour, its owner, Joe Blake, waddled out of the kitchen wiping his greasy hands on his apron and wearing a sloppy and open smile. "Well, Custis, we haven't seen you in here for at least two days! Welcome back."

"Thanks, Joe."

"What will it be tonight?"

"Pork chops, baked potato, and whatever fresh bread that you've baked today as well as a slice of fresh apple pie for dessert."

"You've got it. How about a beer, or would you rather have a shot of whiskey or glass of the house's special wine?"

"Last time I drank your special house wine I got the all-night shits so I'll have a couple shots of whiskey and water."

Joe Blake laughed. He was a big man, fat and jolly. Joe and his equally fat and jolly wife, Lucy, were doing a terrific business since opening up only six months earlier. In addition to Joe's secret sauces, Lucy was a marvel at making fresh fruit pies, especially apple and cherry. Sometimes they had some hired help when the place was full, but mostly the couple was doing every-thing on their own to maximize their profits. Joe had once confided to Longarm that he and Lucy had their sights on buying a larger restaurant building and they were saving their money to that end.

Joe leaned close to Longarm and whispered so that Lucy couldn't hear from the kitchen, "I've got a new gal coming in to interview for a part-time job in the evening when we have our dinner rush. And wait until you catch a look at her!"

"Pretty easy on the eyes?"

Joe rolled his own eyes around. "She's so delicious to look at that I'm afraid Lucy won't dare let me hire her, but she would draw crowds of men. Probably double my business."

"She sounds like the one to hire," Longarm said. "Lucy isn't worried about you falling for a young, beautiful woman is she?"

"Oh, we're fat and getting old but she still keeps a close eye on this fat old alley cat," Joe confessed with a boisterous laugh. "Oh, she is coming up the sidewalk right now!"

Joe dashed into the kitchen to remove his apron, wipe the sweat off his face, and comb his hair. Longarm didn't want to gawk so he pretended to study the menu until the woman opened the door and stepped up to the counter.

From the corner of his eye, Longarm could see that Joe had not exaggerated about this woman's looks. She was probably in her early thirties with long black hair and dark eyes. Her complexion was olive and her figure was that of a Greek goddess.

"Hello!" she called over the counter and into the kitchen.

Joe came out with his pudgy, sweating wife. "Thanks for coming back."

"I hope you've decided to hire me. I need the money and I'm ready to go to work right now."

Joe grinned from ear to ear and his whole body jiggled with excitement, but Lucy who had crowded in behind him didn't crack even a hint of a smile.

"Sure you can," Joe gushed.

But Lucy shook her head and three chins. "Miss, I'm afraid that we really can't afford to hire on any new help right now. Maybe in a few weeks, but not now."

The woman sighed and her eyes went back and forth between the couple. But instead of walking out, she gave it one more try. "Ma'am, your husband said you really needed some help in the evenings and I'm experienced."

"I've no doubt about that," Lucy said, her voice clipped and cool. "But I'm afraid we just can't use you."

"I'm really good with customers. You don't even have to pay me a wage if you let me keep the tips. I promise I'll never steal from your cash register and I'll work hard."

Joe turned to his wife with pleading in her eyes. "Lucy, she's just what we need and she'll be great for our business."

"We'll talk about it later," Lucy snapped.

"Does that mean that you might change your mind?" the woman asked.

"Sure, we might," Joe gushed. "Could you come back tomorrow about this same time?"

"If it makes a difference." She looked right into Lucy's eyes. "I'm a respectable person and I'll be good for your restaurant business, ma'am. You don't have to worry about me doing anything wrong."

It seemed clear as a bell to Longarm that this woman was telling Lucy Butler that she would not entice or manipulate her husband Joe based on her looks and luscious figure.

"Come back tomorrow ready to work," Lucy finally said. "We'll give you a shift or two and see how it goes you workin' only for tips."

The woman smiled. "Thank you." Then, giving Longarm an equally broad smile, she said, "Good-bye."

Joe called, "If you're a little short on money, would you like something to eat before the dinner crowd arrives?"

"What?" she asked, turning at the open door.

"I mean, maybe it would be good to have you sort of watch how we operate here at the Sizzling Pig and taste a few of our specialty dishes."

"Thank you, but . . ."

"I could use some company," Longarm offered, coming to his feet. "How about I treat you to a nice supper?"

"And why would you do that for a complete stranger?" she asked with surprising bluntness.

"I don't like to eat alone and I do enjoy attractive female company. Is that honest enough?"

"His name is Marshal Custis Long," Joe offered. "He's a gentleman."

Her eyes took his full measure as she carefully weighed his words. "Yes, Marshal, it is," she finally decided while taking a chair opposite him. "And to be equally honest, I'm *starved* and I have a very healthy appetite."

"So this is going to cost me plenty."

"Yeah, it will. Want to take back your offer?"

"No," Longarm said, watching Joe try to push his heavy wife into the kitchen and out of listening range. "How about we start with some whiskey?"

"I'd rather have a glass of good wine."

"Trust me," Longarm said, lowering his voice, "you don't want their special house wine."

"And why is that?"

"It'll give you the green apple quickstep."

For a moment, she didn't quite get it and then she burst into hearty laughter. "Well, thanks for the warning, Marshal!"

"Custis, Custis Long at your service."

"My name is Natalia Young." She extended her hand across the table and added, "I've just arrived in Denver and work at the millinery shop two blocks from here. It doesn't pay very well so I need some extra income and Mr. Blake said that I could work here most evenings for a few hours. But . . . I'm not sure that his wife is going to go along with that."

"Lucy will come around," Longarm replied. "Those two are as close as two peas in a pod, and Joe wouldn't think of hurting or betraying his wife."

"I'm glad to hear you say that. I've . . . I've had some problems in the past with that sort of thing."

"Looking at you that is easy to believe."

"You're a pretty good-looking man yourself, Marshal."

"Custis."

"All right then, we'll use our first names. What are you ordering?"

Longarm told her and she said, "I'll have the same. And if the wine isn't too healthy, how about whiskey?"

"That's what I'm drinking."

Natalia nodded. "I think I'm going to enjoy you almost as much as eating those pork chops."

"Probably even more," Longarm said as he signaled for Joe to bring him the whiskey.

Their dinner was delicious and the whiskey was, if not first rate, certainly not to be complained about. They both had big slices of apple pie and then Longarm paid the bill.

"Joe?" he called over the crowd that had begun to fill the room, "this bill seems a little light to me."

"If it is, then it's the only thing light around this place," Joe called. "See you tomorrow about five, Natalia?"

"As soon as I get off my other job at the millinery store I'll hurry right over."

"See you then!"

Longarm paid the bill, which Lucy collected at the counter after mumbling, "It's a wonder my husband's generosity hasn't already sent us both to the poorhouse."

"Here," Longarm said, giving Lucy an extra two dollars. "Your apple pie was worth the price of the whole dinner all by itself."

Lucy's scowl turned into a big smile. "You're so full of horseshit, Custis. A real charmer. Natalia, you'd better watch out because you are with a very smooth-talking man."

"I learned that the minute I sat down at his table."

"I'm just warning you is all," Lucy said. "Watch Custis like a fox."

"I will."

Outside on the sidewalk, Natalia burst into laughter. "She just said you were full of horseshit!"

"Only half full."

Natalia took his arm. "Where do you live?"

"Just up the street three blocks. Where do you live?"

"Nowhere in particular yet."

"Want to see my apartment and my ugly old alley cat?"

"Sounds good. I don't suppose you'd have any more whiskey? Just a shot or two?"

"I just happen to have whiskey and it's a damn sight better than what we just drank at the Sizzling Pig."

"Then let's go sample some and get better acquainted."

Longarm thought that was about the best idea he'd heard all day. And suddenly, he was kind of hoping that he wouldn't be heading off to Cheyenne in the morning.

Chapter 3

Longarm had an old horsehair couch and it was covered with newspapers, so he brushed them aside and said, "Have a seat and I'll get that whiskey and a couple of glasses."

"Thank you. Nice place you have here, but it looks as if it could stand a little housecleaning."

"Yeah, I sure dislike doing that."

"Where is the alley cat you told me about?"

Longarm opened the window to his cramped second-story apartment and hollered, "Hey, George!"

Moments later a huge yellow-striped tabby appeared at the window and then jumped lightly into the room. "George, meet Natalia."

The big cat jumped onto the couch and then into Natalia's lap and began to purr. "Why, he's a big darling!"

"I like him," Longarm admitted. "When I'm gone I leave the window open a crack so he can come inside and eat. When I found him in the alley out back he was just skin and bones but I've fattened him up and now he eats as much as a lot of dogs."

"Is he house-trained?"

"Sure is. George does his business down in the alley. He keeps himself pretty clean and he doesn't make much of a bother."

Natalia took her drink from Longarm and raised it in a toast. "To you and to me."

"And to George," he added, "and to success at your new job tomorrow at the Sizzling Pig."

Natalia took a gulp and sighed with appreciation. "This is pretty good whiskey, Custis."

"Glad you approve."

He sat down next to her and leaned back against the sagging cushion. "So how do you like Denver?"

"If I can survive and make ends meet, I'll like it very much. It's a safe and attractive city and I'd love to venture into those Rocky Mountains someday. I'll bet it's beautiful up there."

"It is," Longarm agreed. "I've seen most of it and it never fails to leave me with a sense of peace and wonder."

"I suppose you've traveled a lot in your work."

"I have. I've been all over the West and seen the good of it and the bad. Colorado is my favorite place, but Montana and Wyoming are pretty spectacular. And I've been down in the Grand Canyon and that's something you can never forget. And not far from it there is a patch of desert that is as colorful as an artist's palette."

"I'd like to see all of that someday."

"Working two jobs and getting a lot of tips should allow you to save up for some vacations."

"That's my plan."

"No children or husband?"

"I left my husband several years ago back in Vermont. He was a very successful businessman, but a very unsuccessful husband."

"How so?"

Natalia blushed. "He not only liked other women . . . but also other men."

"Oh." Longarm took a hasty drink. "I guess that happens."

"I'll bet that you have liked and loved plenty of women in your time," Natalia said, watching him closely.

"I have."

"But you've never settled on one."

Longarm shook his head. "I almost tied the knot a time or two, but . . ."

"But what?"

He shrugged. "I'm just not the marrying or settling down kind and my work takes me out of town a lot. Wouldn't be fair to take a wife and father children and not be around. And there is the danger part of it, and I'd not want to leave a widow and fatherless children."

"That makes sense," Natalia agreed, stroking George who looked as if he were perfectly content to spend the evening in her lap and was purring up a storm.

Longarm reached out and took the cat from Natalia then carried him to the window. "Sorry, old buddy, but you're going to have to take a walk for a while."

Natalia cocked her head. "What did you do that for?"

"He likes to watch."

"Watch *what*?"

"You know what I'm talking about," Longarm said as he took the woman in his arms and kissed her mouth. "Dirty old George likes to sit on the bed as close as he can get and watch every move. And sometimes, just at the very worst time, he starts caterwauling."

"Oh my gosh, that would be . . . distracting."

Longarm slipped his hand around and began to undress Natalia while she reached down and unbuttoned his fly.

"I haven't seen your bedroom yet," she breathed into this ear.

"I thought we might start out right here on the couch."

"You're the boss," she whispered, starting to work at his belt.

They undressed each other quickly and Longarm clucked his tongue in appreciation. "My, oh, my, Natalia, you are quite an eyeful."

She took his already stiffening manhood and stroked its head. "And you're a *bull* of a man."

Longarm eased Natalie back on his couch, then lifted her leg and placed her heel up on the top of the backrest. He climbed onto the couch between her legs and rubbed his stiff rod against her bush until she began to squirm with desire.

"Oh, my goodness," she moaned. "If you ever get started, it's going to be really nice!"

He pushed his rod into her wet pubis and found the spot he was looking for to enter. Slowly, ever so slowly he entered Natalia until he was in her all the way.

"You fill me up and then some," she panted, cocking the upraised leg over his back.

"I haven't even begun to fill you up," he grunted as

he began to thrust slowly at first and then with increasing urgency.

Natalie wrapped both of her legs around his pounding hips and her mouth formed a circle of pleasure as he rode her hard.

"My God!" she cried. "You were telling the truth!"

"About what?" he gasped.

"About George! He's glued up against that window staring at us."

"He's a pervert," Longarm grunted, giving the tomcat a murderous glance.

"Let him watch," she moaned. "At this point, I don't care about anything other than what you are doing to me."

Longarm growled down in his throat and he took her like a lion . . . or like a big alley cat might take a whining female feline in heat.

Natalia was sound asleep when Longarm hastily finished dressing and headed out the door. He'd come back later in the morning to see her and hurriedly pack a small leather satchel he kept for traveling.

When he arrived at the office, Billy was already sipping his first cup of coffee. When he saw the bags under Longarm's eyes he shook his head. "Looks like you had a typically hard night."

"Not so hard," Longarm replied. "I met a new lady at the Sizzling Pig and we hit it off quite well."

Billy snorted with derision. "I'm sure you did."

"She's really nice and not bad-looking, either. Her name is Natalia and she's going to be working the evening dinner shift at the Sizzling Pig."

"I haven't taken the missus there for a while. Maybe I'll take her tonight just out of curiosity and take a gander at your latest love."

"Don't mention my name or Natalia will be embarrassed in front of the other customers."

"I wouldn't dare think of doing that," Billy said, handing Longarm a message. "Take this on over to the telegraph office and have them send it right away. If you can, hang around because I expect a fast reply."

"I'll get some *good* coffee instead of this goat piss you're drinking and some breakfast besides."

"The northbound train leaves a little after eleven this morning for Cheyenne. It keeps to its schedule so be on time and be ready."

"I will."

Longarm took the message and headed for the telegraph office, which happened to be near the Frontier Hotel. After sending the message he decided to have breakfast at the Frontier in the hope of seeing Miss St. Clair for a few minutes just to inquire how she was feeling. Longarm felt a trifle guilty of doing so after last night with Natalia, but he had made it pretty clear that he was not looking for a deep or serious relationship. Trouble was that most women that he took to bed always seemed to want to wiggle their way deeper and deeper into his life. Hopefully, Natalia would be different.

After leaving the telegraph office and telling the operator that he'd be back in an hour to see if there was a return message, Longarm headed straight for the Frontier Hotel.

"Good morning," he said, mustering up as much

cheerfulness as a man could muster after an all-night sexual bonanza. "I'd like to have breakfast and see if Miss St. Clair is up and about."

"Miss who?"

"Miss St. Clair. She is Mr. John Holt's niece. She's staying up on the top floor and is the one whose father just died in a tragic accident on Colfax."

"Mr. Holt and his staff require the entire top floor," the desk clerk said, checking his register. "But I really don't know anything about a Miss St. Clair or remember hearing about the death of her father. Are you sure they were *our* guests?"

"Of course I'm sure! Look, why don't you call the manager over here."

"But I . . ."

Longarm showed the flustered clerk his marshal's badge. "I want to see the manager right now."

He cooled his heels in the lobby, barely paying attention to the fine artwork on the walls or the impressive rugs and chandeliers. Ten minutes passed and then an impeccably well-dressed man of some bearing in his forties appeared at his side. "Is there some misunderstanding, Marshal?"

"Yes, there is. Yesterday I escorted a very shaken young woman named Miss Lilly St. Clair to this hotel. Now, your dim-witted desk clerk says he has no knowledge of this woman."

The man smiled and tipped the palms of his soft hands upward in supplication. "And I'm afraid, Marshal, neither do I."

Longarm's jaw dropped. "There has to be some

mistake! This woman was quite beautiful with long, dark blond hair and she was about five foot eight. When I dropped her off she had a bandage on her cheek and . . ."

"Are you certain that you have the right hotel?"

"Of course I'm sure!" Longarm shouted with exasperation.

"I'm very sorry, Marshal, but there is no such person registered at this hotel."

Suddenly, Longarm spotted an old man being helped toward the dining room by an only slightly younger old man. "Mr. Holt!" he called, hurrying after the gentleman.

John Holt had to be in his late eighties and although he walked with a shuffle and was hard of hearing, there was nothing wrong with his memory or his mind.

"Marshal Custis Long," he said, smiling and extending his blue-veined hand. "How good to see you again! What a nice surprise. Would you join me at breakfast and tell me all the latest adventures that you've enjoyed since last we talked?"

"Well . . . well, sure, Mr. Holt. I'd be honored to share your company but first I have to ask you if you have a niece by the name of Lilly St. Clair."

His face lit up with pleasure. "Of course I do! She is one of the dearest souls on earth."

Longarm heaved a sigh of relief. "And I understand that she and her father are staying here at your hotel and . . ."

"Why," Holt said, expression changing, "if Lilly is here it is news to me and the Sisters of Mercy."

"What?"

"Lilly St. Clair took her vows years ago and is a nun

at a convent in New York. I haven't seen the dear woman since she was a child although she and I have regularly corresponded over the years. I've been a benefactor to her and her convent and we do hope to meet again someday."

Longarm felt as if he had been struck dumb. "What does Miss St. Clair look like?"

"Sister St. Clair?" Holt shook his head. "I really have no idea. She was about twelve years old the last time I saw her and although she was very sweet, she was certainly not attractive. Pudgy, buckteeth, and freckles. Very religious. Wonderful sense of humor and kind heart. Even back then she knew she wanted to become a nun and devote her life to God and to those among us less fortunate."

Before Longarm could even drudge up a reply, the old man and his almost equally old and frail manservant moved into the dining room. "Come along, Marshal, we have so much to talk about you and me!"

"Mr. Holt," Longarm muttered to himself, "you don't even know the half of it."

Longarm was in a bit of a daze while the old man talked and fielded questions about the economy, Denver politics, and the hotel business. Forty-five minutes and a splendid breakfast that Longarm barely tasted passed before he asked the old gentleman. "I met a woman named Miss St. Clair yesterday."

"You did!" Holt grinned. "I wonder if they are related. Did she have red hair and freckles?"

"No, this woman would be in her late twenties or early thirties with long, ash-blond hair. She was quite beautiful but scratched up a bit and shaken from a serious buggy-overturning accident."

"My, my! It certainly doesn't sound as if she could be any blood relation to my dear Sister Lilly."

"No, it doesn't." Longarm took a final sip of coffee. "This Lilly St. Clair said she and her father were staying on the top floor of this hotel."

"Impossible."

"So I understand. Did you see a woman and an older man anywhere in the hotel?"

"How old is the man?"

"Sixties and he died in the accident yesterday."

"How sad. Maybe there is some blood relationship between your Miss St. Clair and my dear Sister St. Clair."

"Somehow I very much doubt it."

"Well," John Holt said, dabbing the biscuit crumbs from his gray mustache and standing. "I really enjoyed having breakfast with you and I do hope you find the Miss St. Clair that you met yesterday. If you do, please ask her if she has a sister in New York that is a nun."

"I'll do that." Longarm stood. "Oh, Mr. Holt?"

"Yes?"

"If you do meet this woman, I would like you to let me know about it. Could you send someone over to the Federal Building and if I'm not there have them ask for a Marshal Vail."

Holt looked to his manservant. "Can you remember that, Willard?"

"Yes, sir. I think I can."

"Good." He turned back to Longarm. "Very nice

seeing you again, Marshal. Just pay for your breakfast at the desk if you please."

"Yes, sir."

No wonder the old man was so damn wealthy, Longarm thought as he followed him out of the dining room to pay his breakfast bill.

Chapter 4

Longarm returned to the telegraph office and a message was handed to him that read:

DEPUTY U.S. MARSHAL ST. CLAIR STILL MISSING STOP FEAR DEAD STOP

Longarm stared at the message in shock. He reread it again.

"Sounds bad, I'm afraid," the telegraph operator said. "Maybe that marshal was shot to death hunting for those train robbers."

"Yeah," Longarm quietly agreed as he headed back to his office.

When he showed Billy Vail the telegram, his boss shook his head. "I didn't know the man's last name. Say, isn't that the same name as . . ."

"That's right," Longarm replied. "The woman who was in that overturned carriage was named Lilly St. Clair and she's vanished."

"What do you mean, 'vanished'?"

Longarm shrugged. "After the accident I took her to the mortuary and then to the Frontier Hotel where I left her at the steps. She was badly shaken and I thought it best that she get her rest. But when I returned to the hotel this morning, they didn't know a thing about her."

"How odd," Billy said. "Perhaps you got a desk clerk who—"

"No," Longarm interrupted. "I spoke to the desk clerk's superior and he confirmed that there had not been a Mrs. St. Clair registered at that hotel. And then, I even met the hotel's owner and had breakfast with the old gentleman."

"That would be Mr. Holt. How is he doing, by the way?"

"He's pretty frail but still mentally sharp. I asked him about Lilly St. Clair and he said that is the name of his niece, who is a nun."

"A nun?"

"Yep. She's in some convent in New York and he hasn't seen her in years. Mr. Holt thought that there had to be some confusion on my part, and I have to admit that I *am* damned confused!"

Billy leaned back in his office chair and scowled. "I don't know what to tell you, Custis. This is all very peculiar. It hardly seems possible that there are two women named Lilly St. Clair. That's not exactly a common last name."

"I know that."

Billy waved his hand as if to dismiss the confusion from his mind. "Why don't you just forget about this Lilly St. Clair and concentrate on Deputy U.S. Marshal

St. Clair, who is missing since going after train robbers out of Cheyenne."

"I can do that," Longarm replied, "but something is very wrong about this whole situation."

"Perhaps when you get to Cheyenne and speak to the marshal up there you'll be able to solve this mystery."

"I'm going to make it a point to do that," Longarm vowed.

"You'd better get packed and moving or you'll miss the train."

"I know that."

"I'll meet you at the station with your round-trip ticket in hand and some travel money from this office."

"Good." Longarm headed for the door. "Oh, and Billy?"

"Yes."

"This time give me at least a hundred dollars so that if I have to rent a horse and provision myself for a manhunt, I'll have enough funds."

"Don't I always give you enough?"

"Never," Longarm said. "The last time I was out you gave me such a miserly travel advance that I had to eat beans and drink cheap whiskey during most meals."

"Sorry," Billy said, not looking sorry at all. "But you do travel more than anyone else in this office and I do have a *limited* budget."

"Just bring a hundred dollars minimum," Longarm demanded. "What I don't spend on legitimate travel expenses I'll return."

"Sure you will!" Billy guffawed. "When hell freezes over!"

Longarm sighed with resignation and hurried out to get his bags and then meet his boss at the train station. He had maybe a half hour to spare and he could use that time to buy a few necessities for the trip up to Cheyenne. Things were always cheaper here in Denver, and given his measly travel advances, it was important to cut his costs.

Natalia was cooking breakfast when he returned dressed only in one of his long-sleeved shirts. "Hello," she said with a wide smile. "I was counting on you to return and figured you would be hungry."

"I already had a big breakfast at the Frontier Hotel. Just came back to grab my bag and a few things I'll need on the trip north."

Natalia came over and planted a big kiss on his lips. She unbuttoned his shirt and smiled. "I hope you at least have a few minutes for a loving good-bye."

"Holy Hanna," he breathed, licking his lips. "You sure know how to change a man's mind."

Natalia took his hand and led him to his bedroom. She lay down on the bed and whispered, "Let's not waste any more time on just words."

Longarm was still tired and drained from the night-long love fest that they'd enjoyed but just the sight of her lying there waiting made his manhood stand up at attention. In seconds, he was out of his clothes and making love to Natalia and it was every bit as passionate as it had been the evening before. When at last he emptied his seed and went limp, Natalia gave her hips a few final and powerful thrusts and then moaned with pleasure, signifying that she had been satisfied as well.

Longarm forced himself to stand and then use the washbasin to clean himself off. "I'll be back as soon as I can and you can stay here while I'm gone. Just take care of George and enjoy yourself."

"After what we just did, it will be hard to do that and George certainly isn't going to take your place."

"I'd hope not." Longarm chuckled as he stuffed things into his satchel. "Oh, and good luck with your new job."

"I'm going to like working there in the evenings."

"Don't bring any customers up here for dessert."

"I wouldn't dream of it!" she cried, sounding offended.

"I wonder."

Longarm leaned over and kissed both of her nipples and then her mouth. "You taste good all over."

"Sure you don't want just a little more of me before you go?" she asked enticingly.

"If I had any more of you, Natalia, I'd probably pass out from weakness."

"Ha!"

Longarm blew her a kiss at the doorway and then he was rushing to the train station.

Billy was pacing up and down the platform and looking upset. "Well there you are, finally! The train is almost read to pull out and I thought sure you were going to miss it."

"Nope. I'm here and I'm ready."

Billy shook his head. "Why don't you tuck in your shirt and button up your pants, Marshal."

Longarm blushed with embarrassment. "Good idea."

"All right," Billy said. "I want a telegram as soon as you've visited the town marshal telling me what you intend to do."

"I'm going to find out why we suddenly have three people named St. Clair," Longarm told the man.

"Just . . . just find the missing federal marshal so that I can report to my Washington, DC, bosses that we've taken care of the problem."

"I'll do that," Longarm vowed, jumping onto the train as it jerked forward and started up the tracks.

"And try not to get all the single women in Cheyenne pregnant!" Billy roared.

Longarm stood on the platform between the two cars and buttoned his fly, then he entered the coach and collapsed in an empty seat. He knew that he must look like something the cat dragged in after a long, hard night but he didn't really care. He would close his eyes and soon be sound asleep. By the time this train pulled into Cheyenne, he would feel like a new man.

Chapter 5

Cheyenne, the territorial capital of Wyoming, was a railroad and a cow town in that order of importance. A large sign tacked on the wall beside the railroad depot let arrivals know that the town had been founded by Maj. Gen. Grenville Dodge in 1867. Cheyenne had soon become a crossroads of sort, a big railroad repair site and a major loading depot for grass-fed cattle headed for the eastern stockyards and packing houses.

Longarm had often thought that, if Denver represented a solid, middle-aged father, then Cheyenne was his wild and rebellious teenage son. The town was booming but it didn't have the cobblestone streets or older and often elegant homes with big trees and nice sidewalks. There were no sidewalks in Cheyenne except for its downtown area where there were more saloons than restaurants and more whorehouses than churches.

Longarm enjoyed the wide-open and devil-may-care feeling and knew that it had been named after the

Cheyenne Indians and its nickname was "Hell on Wheels." He doubted he would have liked being one of its local law officers, but as far as the spirit and excitement of the place, it could hardly be matched. Cowboys rode their horses recklessly through the downtown and if one of them had a bit too much to drink and fired a few shots into the sky, well, that was to be expected when hardworking men came into town to let off some steam.

The railroad workers were more sober, but not much. They tended to dress differently in bib overalls and not be nearly as free spending or boisterous. Many of them were older men and they wore grease and soot on their clothing as their badges of honor. They had more stability and larger paychecks but weren't nearly as fun loving as the wild young cowboys. In addition to those two different and often fist-fighting factions, there were merchants, Indians, squinty-eyed and soft-handed gamblers, whores, some dry-land farmers and homesteaders as well as a few professionals like doctors, lawyers, and federal law officers. Whenever Longarm came up from Denver he was always surprised to see that a lot of the businesses he remembered on his previous trip had gone out of business and their places were taken by new entrepreneurs filled with hope. Had it not been for the railroad, Cheyenne wouldn't have existed, but no one told the cowboys that fact and ended standing upright.

"Well, Marshal Long," the Union Pacific supervisor said when Longarm hopped down from the train. "Good to see you again!"

"Well, thank you, Lloyd. Always nice to see a smiling face and a change of scenery."

"You going on to Laramie or maybe even as far as Reno tomorrow on our train?"

"Nope. I expect that this will be the end of the line for me this trip."

"Well, enjoy yourself. The Red Garter Bar and Café has been taken over by new owners and they serve up as good a pot roast as you've ever tasted. They barbecue their steaks and beef ribs on a grill fired by wood and sagebrush and put a special sauce on 'em so they're tender enough to melt in your mouth."

"That's good to know. Thanks for the tip."

Lloyd was a hefty fellow and he patted his stomach. "Lordy, if I ate more than once a week at the Red Garter, I'd weigh three hundred pounds instead of only two! I'd be so fat that I wouldn't be able to climb on and off this train without getting stuck in the doorway."

Longarm laughed and headed into town. He had long ago established his favorite haunts and eateries, but he decided he would try the Red Garter and a big steak sounded just about right after the railroad ride up from Denver. But first, he supposed he ought to stop in at the local marshal's office and get the latest report on that missing lawman.

Hell, he thought, maybe the man had just gotten lost somewhere out in the sticks or decided to quit being a marshal and take up another and safer line of work. It had happened plenty of times before and it wouldn't be surprising if it had happened this time as well.

Still, there was the puzzle of the missing Lilly St. Clair and the unlikely coincidence of the missing marshal with the same last name. Longarm, being a highly curious man, was eager to clear up that mystery. And while he wasn't eager to return to a desk in Denver, the downside of that would be more than offset by the company of the lovely and damned near insatiable Natalia. Just thinking about that woman made his pulse pound a little faster and when he pulled out his pocket watch and saw that it was about this time that she would be going on her first early evening shift at the Sizzling Pig, he could well imagine that the young male customers would be salivating over a whole lot more than their upcoming delicious cooked pork.

The marshal's office was on Capitol Avenue and the last time that Longarm had visited, a new man named Charlie Oatman had been promoted to become Cheyenne's chief marshal after his predecessor had been gunned down by a pair of drunken mule skinners.

Pushing the door open, Longarm smiled and recognized the newly appointed marshal sitting behind his desk. "Good to see you again, Marshal Oatman. I understand that a federal officer is missing."

"That's right. He's not on my payroll so it doesn't matter too much to me if he comes or goes, but I was sure that your office would want to investigate."

Longarm took a chair and a cup of black coffee that was offered. Oatman was young, probably still in his late twenties, and he seemed to be both smart and professional. Longarm had known the man's father before he'd died and the senior Oatman had also been a law officer.

"How was the ride up from Denver?" Oatman began, sipping his coffee and then rolling a cigarette.

"It doesn't change much," Longarm replied. "I usually take the opportunity to get a good nap."

Oatman lit his cigarette and blew a cloud of smoke over their heads. "You think that I could get on with the federal marshal's office in Denver sometime?"

Longarm hadn't been expecting that question but it was easy enough to answer. "We're always looking for experienced lawmen. However, I think your chances would be much better if you got a year here as chief marshal under your belt before applying with us."

"A year in my chair in this wild-assed town can seem like a lifetime," Oatman replied. "But I see your point and I'll try to do a good job here before I apply with your office in Denver."

"What can you tell me about the missing federal marshal named St. Clair?" Longarm asked.

"He wasn't here for long. I'm not sure who sent him or if he really had an assignment. I can tell you he was different."

"How so?"

Oatman frowned. "Well, he was always asking questions about the business people here in Cheyenne. Questions that I thought were really none of his business. And when I'd ask him why he wanted to know answers that seemed to be personal, he'd get defensive."

"Did he do anything?"

"Marshal Link St. Clair liked to hang out with the most prominent people in town."

"On a *lawman's* salary?" Longarm asked with skepticism. "How could he afford to do that?"

"Link obviously had plenty of money. Once, when we

went out and had a few too many beers, Link confessed that he'd made quite a lot of money and judging from the looks of his wife and the clothes that she wore, I believed him. When I asked Link why he had pinned on a federal marshal's badge, he told me that he'd learned money wasn't everything in life and he liked the danger."

"Describe his wife."

"She was beautiful. Average height and light blond hair." Oatman tilted his head back and stared at the ceiling for a moment. "I'll be real honest with you, Custis, when Mrs. Lilly St. Clair walked down the street, she was so striking that men would stop and stare . . . even the old and the married ones."

"I met her for a few hours," Longarm told the marshal. "Did she have an elderly father?"

"Yeah. Nice old guy, but he wasn't in good health. I understand he had quite a bit of money, and I had the impression that he wasn't all that fond of the man that his daughter had married so he watched over her pretty closely."

"Her father have a real fancy carriage pulled by an exceptionally good-looking and matched pair of sorrels?"

"Sure did. Haven't seen them around town for a while, though."

"The carriage was a runaway in downtown Denver and was demolished when it overturned. The old man was killed and Lilly was pretty badly shaken and banged up."

"My gawd!" Charlie leaned forward in his office chair. "I'll bet that's where Link St. Clair took off for! He's in Denver but . . ."

"I never saw the man and she said her husband was dead." Longarm stroked the waxed tips of his handlebar mustache. "I'll tell you the truth, Charlie; this whole situation has me completely flummoxed."

"Well, you need to go back to Denver and talk to Lilly. I'll bet when you find her you'll also find Link."

"Somehow, I don't think so."

The chief marshal blinked and then looked closely at Longarm. "Is there something that you're not telling me?"

"Lilly told me that her uncle owned the Frontier Hotel. Yet, when I met the man he said that he did have a niece named Lilly St. Clair but that she was a nun."

"What!"

Longarm threw up his hands in resignation. "I'm just telling you what I know. Lilly disappeared just like her husband."

Charlie Oatman took a few minutes to digest all of this information and then he said, "I think we ought to go out to their ranch and see if anyone can put an end to this confusion."

"They have a ranch?" Longarm asked with surprise.

"Oh, yeah. A real nice one, too. I told you that Link made no real secret that he had pinned on a badge out of boredom rather than necessity."

"How far out is this ranch?"

"About five or six miles." Oatman finished his smoke and stood up. "You ready now or would you like to get checked into a hotel and get something to eat?"

"We've got a few hours before dark. Let's get out there and see if we can get to the bottom of this mess. I do assume you've already gone out there before you sent us a telegram about Link's disappearance."

"I did but the place was locked up and no one was around."

"Well," Longarm said, "did you enter the house?"

"Nope. I thought that, if I broke a window or door in it would be overstepping my bounds. I had no reason to think that anything was seriously wrong. Given that Link and his fine-looking wife had money, I figured they might have just gone away for a while on business or pleasure."

"They have any dogs or horses?"

"Not a one."

"That's odd," Longarm said. "I don't know if I've ever been to a ranch that didn't at least have a dog to sound the alarm when unexpected visitors suddenly appeared."

"I'd never been out to the St. Clair place before," Oatman admitted. "But I could see everything there cost plenty of money."

"I'll need a horse and saddle," Longarm said.

"I've got both you can borrow."

"Then let's ride," Longarm told the younger man. "I'm about to burst out of curiosity."

"Wouldn't it be something if both Link and his wife, Lilly, are just sitting on the porch with a mint julep when we go fogging up to their ranch expecting the worst?"

"We'll ride up just like we're sightseeing," Longarm told the man. "I've been made a fool of too many times to make it easy for the couple if there isn't anything wrong."

Chief Marshal Charlie Oatman nodded with agreement. "If they are at home, then they'd better have some ready answers to a lot of questions."

"You got that one right," Longarm said as he headed out the door with his mind full of unanswered questions.

"Did Mrs. St. Clair bury her father in Denver?"

"I don't know. She vanished before he could be put in the ground."

"You mean she just left her father's corpse in a mortuary and took off?"

"That's what it looks like."

Oatman shook his head. "I'd have thought she had better breeding and class than to do a sorry thing like that to her father. They were obviously very close, those two. Link told me he wished that the old man would just move away and quit meddling in his marriage."

"Link St. Clair said that?" Longarm asked with surprise.

"Yep."

Longarm's brow furrowed. He'd been so concerned about Lilly's condition right after the carriage had overturned that he'd not even taken more than a cursory look at Lilly's father. He remembered her saying that he'd had a bad heart and that would certainly have accounted for the runaway and the accident that immediately followed.

But what if the old man hadn't really died of heart failure? What if . . . what if he'd died because of an entirely different reason?

Longarm ground his teeth in frustration. It seemed like the more he learned about the missing Lilly and Link St. Clair, the more perplexing everything seemed.

"I don't actually own two horses," Charlie was saying. "I just have a pair that I rent."

"Doesn't matter to me as long as they're not pokey."

"Oh," Charlie Oatman promised, "that's the last word I'd ever use to describe these boys."

Longarm probably should have asked what the man was talking about but all of his thoughts were focused on what they might find on a ranch only eight miles away.

Chapter 6

"They're out in the back corral," the bent old peg-legged man said, spitting a stream of tobacco between Longarm and the marshal of Cheyenne. "I just grained those big boys so you might want to wait until they're finished."

"No time for that today," Oatman said. "Go fetch us halters and we'll catch them up and bring 'em out for saddlin'."

"All right, but they won't be happy givin' up their oats. They know the minute they walk away from 'em the other horses will eat them oats up."

Longarm scowled. "Mister, we're in a hurry and we need horses *now*, not when the damn things have decided they've eaten their fill."

The stable owner shot Longarm a go-to-hell look and hobbled off to get the halters. Longarm shook his head. "He sure isn't a very friendly sort."

"Arnie thinks a lot of his horses and he keeps them in good shape. These two geldings are brothers. Paint horses, tall and fast."

"Good," Longarm said. "Let's go have a look at them. Arnie can bring the halters out to us."

"Sure thing."

Longarm had no reason to own a horse in Denver. Most of his work was out of town and while he liked and thought he was a pretty good judge of horseflesh, he would prefer to ride a train or take a woman out for a buggy ride any day.

"There they are," Oatman said. "They're nothing much to look at, but I think you'll like the way they move if you're in a hurry."

Longarm stared at the pair of paints in utter disbelief and finally whispered, "By gawd, they remind me of a couple of *giraffes*!"

"Aw, they ain't *that* bad-looking."

"Like hell they aren't," Longarm snapped. "They must stand eighteen hands if they're an inch! And look at the size of their mulish-looking heads! And their withers remind me of meat cleavers."

"Now, come on, Custis. It isn't like we're going to ride in the Cheyenne Fourth of July parade."

"I know, but those are the ugliest pair of horses I've ever seen in my life. Cripes, Charlie, they're bow-necked, jug-headed and their front legs are knock-kneed and crooked. And what happened to their tails?"

"They have a bad habit of chewing on each other's tails. Arnie says it's a sign of their affection for one another."

Longarm sighed with resignation. "I wouldn't ride up the street on those jug-headed paint horses even if it was pitch-dark." He looked at the marshal. "So tell me the *real* reason we're riding out of Cheyenne on those giraffes."

"They're cheap and fast," Oatman said with no attempt to hide his irritation. "*That's* the reason."

"Well, Charlie, I'll gladly pay an extra dollar for something that at least resembles a horse."

The marshal lowered his voice. "Listen, I'm courtin' Arnie's daughter, you see? And he'd be hurt if we didn't take 'em." The marshal toed the ground. "Come on. It isn't like we're riding all the way down to Denver or up into Montana. The St. Clair ranch is only eight miles out and eight miles back."

Before Longarm could reply, Arnie showed up with the halters. "Go on in and git 'em, boys!"

"This is sure enough a mule halter," Longarm said with disgust.

Arnie flung the halters at Longarm. "Fits 'em just fine. Which one you ridin', today, Charlie?"

"I'll ride Homer. Custis here can ride Hammer."

Longarm wasn't sure he'd heard right. "The one I'm riding is named . . . *Hammer*?"

"Yeah, he has a bit of an iron jaw," Arnie explained with malicious delight.

Longarm and Charlie went into the corral and as soon as they approached the pair that was gobbling up their separate tubs of oats, Homer and Hammer laid back their ears and showed their long, yellow front teeth.

"Now boys," Charlie crooned nervously. "We're just

going for a little ride and you can shore enough eat those oats when you get back tonight."

But when Charlie tried to slip a halter on Homer, the gelding's neck unwound and the paint bit him on the arm so hard that the town marshal howled. Longarm moved in on Hammer and the animal lunged and snapped. That ticked Longarm off so much that he swung the heavy leather halter and belted the big paint across his donkey-like ears.

Hammer shook his immense head and when he showed his teeth, Longarm walloped him again. The paint shook his head, then seemed to accept the fact that he was either going to behave or get beaten. Hammer lowered his head and stepped toward Longarm suddenly as gentle as a lamb.

"Weren't any call to hit him so hard across the damn ears like that!" Arnie snapped from a vantage point safely outside the corral.

Longarm struggled until he had the halter fitted and drawled, "Oh, yes, there was."

The marshal was still bent up in agony holding his forearm so Longarm got the second paint haltered. They led the pair of uglies out to a hitch rail and saddled them without incident.

"Point 'em in the direction you want to go right from the start," Arnie warned. "Because for the first mile or two they think they're racehorses!"

Longarm barely got his right leg over the cantle when Hammer bolted forward and shot out of the livery yard. He twisted around to see the town marshal storming up the street right behind.

"Won't take long to get out to the St. Clair Ranch at this pace!" Marshal Oatman yelled as Homer drew up beside him and the animals raced westward neck and neck.

"If we're still alive to see it," Longarm shouted as he clung to the saddle horn and let his fool paint horse race like the wind.

The St. Clair Ranch was at the end of a grassy valley nestled in between two tall mountains. A clear stream ran through the valley, which was ringed by pine trees. Longarm didn't see any cattle or horses as they rode onto the ranch property and he had an edgy feeling that something was very much amiss.

Where were the livestock? He could see a fine log-built ranch house up ahead and all the barns and outbuildings, and it was immediately apparent that this was not your ordinary hardscrabble operation. All the fences were well strung and the gates didn't sag. The buildings all looked in excellent repair and there was a huge pile of split wood waiting for winter and even a large fenced garden with corn and other vegetables growing tall. Flowers had been planted across the front veranda and there were a couple of good wagons sitting beside a huge hay barn.

"Looks like it's right out of a picture, doesn't it?" Oatman said with admiration. "When the St. Clairs bought the place it was kinda run down. But they had workmen out here for weeks getting it back into shape."

"It's a real nice place," Longarm agreed. "Did they ever have many cowboys on their payroll?"

"Nope. I think they just had an old Chinese cook and

servant and maybe another old man that I'd see riding
into town with the Chinaman to buy supplies."

"So if they don't have any livestock or cowboys,"
Longarm asked, "how did the ranch make them any
money?"

Hammer and Homer had run out of steam about a
mile back and were now content to walk along side by
side. Longarm thought he had never been on such a
rough-gaited horse in his life but he'd also never ridden
a faster one.

"Well," Oatman said, "that's a question that a lot of
us in town have asked ourselves. And the answer is that
I don't think they bought the place to make them money.
Nope. I think that Link and Lilly brought enough money
with them when they came out here to just do what
they wanted to do and not worry."

"I see," Longarm replied, though he really didn't. "I
wonder where all their money came from?"

"No one was bold enough to ask, and I'm sure that
if they had, Link would have told them to mind their
own gawdamn business. And he'd have been justified
in telling them that."

"I guess," Longarm said as they rode up closer to the
wide front veranda and then dismounted. "Anyone
home!"

There was no answer. Nothing moved, and for some
reason that made the hair on the back of Longarm's neck
stand up a little.

"Something is just not right here," Longarm told the
town marshal. "Why don't you go around to the back
and see if you can find a window to peek through. I'll
try the front door and peek into those bigger windows."

"All right, but you probably won't see anything more than I did when I was here about a week ago."

"We need to get inside and look around," Longarm said. "But if there is anyone inside, let's first give them a chance to open the place up."

Charlie Oatman disappeared around the corner of the big log house and Longarm stepped up onto the veranda, drawing his Colt revolver because he had a sense of danger.

He knocked on the front door hard. He called, "Anyone home!"

Nothing but silence.

Longarm eased sideways and peered through the curtained window but the light was too dim inside and he saw nothing.

Charlie came back around. "There is a back door but it's locked."

"Then we've got two choices," Longarm said. "Either kick the door off the hinges or bust out their big front window."

"A door can be fixed. A broken window can't."

Longarm saw the logic and leaned back then gave the door a hard kick. It was solid. He threw his shoulder to the door and it didn't budge.

"To hell with it," he muttered using his gun to smash the front window. "They've obviously got plenty of money."

"Sure wish you hadn't've done that," Oatman complained. "That window will cost fifty dollars or more to replace."

"Be quiet and be ready," Longarm said, ignoring the complaint. "I smell something that I sure don't like."

"And what's that?"

Longarm smashed a few sharp pieces of glass out of his way and climbed into the dark interior, whispering, "Charlie, I hate to tell you this but it's the smell of *death*."

Chapter 7

The dead Chinaman was lying faceup in the kitchen with a bloody butcher knife clenched in his fist and with his eyes fixed sightlessly on the ceiling. "Marshal," Longarm said, holstering his gun and studying the corpse, "it looks like you've got a murder on your hands."

"Yeah," Oatman said stoically. "Looks like the old Chinaman put up a pretty good fight before he went down."

"I'd say so. But whoever did this had a gun and shot him three times from the looks of it. Butcher knife is no match for a bullet."

"What else do you see that might be important?" Oatman asked.

"Nothing. I'd say the Chinaman was in here cooking or preparing a meal when he was confronted. Despite being shot, he seemed to have lived long enough to carve his attacker up a bit before he died."

"We'd better look this place over from top to bottom,"

Oatman said. "Maybe we can find some clues that will tell us who did it."

"Maybe. Let's stay together and search the house room by room. I might miss something you'll see and the other way around."

"I just can't imagine who would do such a thing," Oatman said, wagging his head back and forth. "And I wonder what happened to the other old fella that they employed. I think his name was Otto something."

"Maybe we'll find him as dead as the cook and servant," Longarm said as they moved out of the kitchen and down a hallway.

"First bedroom looks like it was unused," Longarm remarked. "Probably for guests."

"That would be my guess."

The second bedroom obviously belonged to the Chinaman. It was small and very neat. The bed was made up and there were candles and incense on the tables in addition to some kind of small shrine.

"Look at this," Longarm said, stopping after going through the man's drawers. "He had a gun and it looks like a small money pouch."

"Do you think someone robbed him?"

Longarm shrugged. "I'm sure that he was paid for his work. Did you ever see him go into a bank to deposit his earnings?"

"No."

"You might want to see if he was putting his paychecks in the bank," Longarm suggested. "If he wasn't . . . and I suspect that's the case here . . . then he'd have saved his money and it might have added up to a considerable amount. Enough to warrant murdering the Chinaman."

Oatman nodded in agreement. "Let's move on to the next room. It's getting toward dark and if we're going to search this place, we're going to have to hurry."

"This is not the time to hurry," Longarm told the younger man. "If we rush through this and miss an important clue then we may never find out who killed the Chinaman."

But Charlie Oatman was excited and in a rush. "Look, you're obviously more experienced at this. I'm going to do a quick search through the house and then the barns."

Longarm nodded because he had no authority over this man. "Do what you think is best, Marshal."

When Oatman left him to make a quick inspection of the other rooms in the house, Longarm forced himself to remain methodical and deliberate. He spent a few minutes in a library then the dining room before he went on to the other bedrooms. When he entered Lilly St. Clair's bedroom, he stopped and the special scent of her perfume brought back memories. But what struck him most was that Lilly had obviously left in a terrible hurry. Her closets and drawers were open and clothes were scattered on the floor. Her bed was unmade and . . . Longarm paused as the realization struck him . . . *Lilly had slept alone.*

He searched every drawer in the fading light and found nothing of real interest. No letters that would give him some insight into her real background. No financial statements or records. No jewelry, either.

Longarm paused for a few precious minutes and tried to get a sense of the woman and especially of her state of mind just before she had left this room and most likely the ranch in such an obviously frantic state of mind.

Was she the killer? Had she robbed the Chinaman and perhaps her husband and taken anything of value in this house, then rushed off to Denver with her father . . . the very same man that Longarm had watched die on Colfax Avenue?

Or had Lilly been running in terror of her husband or someone else . . . someone who had murdered the Chinaman and wanted to kill her as well?

Longarm closed his eyes, breathing in the dying scent of the beautiful Lilly St. Clair and hoping he might have some kind of insight or inspiration. But nothing came so he left the room in its disarray and found Link St. Clair's separate bedroom.

In contrast to Lilly's room, this one was ornate and well organized. Not Spartan like the Chinaman's room, but very masculine in its artwork and decoration. There was a fine mahogany rifle and gun case that immediately caught Longarm's attention because its glass doors were hanging open and the case was empty.

Longarm went through the man's drawers and found nothing of special interest. He checked the closets and realized that Link St. Clair was a big man like himself. Probably at least six foot four inches tall with wide shoulders. Longarm guessed he had been a fine specimen of manhood and probably very good-looking.

With darkness falling Longarm inspected the last rooms and found nothing of special interest. He was just about to go back to the kitchen for a final look at the corpse when he heard Charlie Oatman shouting from outdoors.

Longarm hurried to the veranda and Charlie trotted up, looking shaken. "I found the old man that I think was named Otto. He was lying out behind the barn and the coyotes had . . . well, they found his body before I did and it isn't pretty."

"Calm down," Longarm said gently. "He was dead when they got to him and he didn't feel or know what happened."

"I know. I know, but no human being should have . . ."

Oatman couldn't finish and Longarm didn't press him for details. He'd see the body soon enough and he'd just deal with the sight. He's seen so many bodies over the years that very few really hit him all that hard anymore. But still, if a man's face had been chewed off, it was something that you never quite forgot.

"Follow me," Oatman said in a small voice.

They trotted out behind the barn and sure enough there was Otto . . . or what looked to have been Otto. Longarm walked over to the man and studied what was remained. He ran his finger across Otto's bloody shirt-front and then saw the slashes on his sleeve. "What do you think happened to him?"

Oatman frowned and was silent for a moment. "Maybe it was Otto that killed the Chinaman and he took those cuts from the butcher knife. He probably robbed the Chinaman and tried to escape but he was so weak from blood loss that he passed out and died here."

"That's a lot of guesswork."

Longarm reached into the man's coat pockets and they

were empty. "If this old fella murdered the Chinaman and died of his knife wounds before he could go anyplace, how come he doesn't have any money on him?"

"Maybe he hid it."

Longarm shook his head. "If he'd have done that, it means he'd have had to return, and I'm sure that would be the last thing he'd ever do."

"You're right," the marshal admitted. "But if this old man didn't kill the Chinaman, who did?"

"Link St. Clair is a good possibility. What we know for sure is that someone else was involved."

"How do you . . ."

"Tracks," Longarm said, pointing them out. "These two dead men were not the only ones on this ranch when the bloodbath occurred."

"But who . . ."

"I don't know yet," Longarm answered. "I can tell you this much . . . one way or the other we are going to find out."

Chief Marshal Charlie Oatman nodded. "I'm sure glad that you're here to help me, Custis. I'd be in way over my head without you."

"Ah, you'd probably do fine. You're smart, honest, and most important of all you take your badge and job seriously. But figuring out these murders isn't going to be easy."

"Would you say that Link St. Clair is our most likely murderer?"

"Yeah," Longarm answered. "But the hell of it is that we haven't a clue where to find him. If he did kill these men then it stands to reason that he'd have left in a hurry and gone somewhere far away."

"Link was smart," Oatman said. "He's the kind of man that would be able to hide his back trail."

"Someone must have seen him somewhere in these parts," Longarm mused aloud. "It'll be my job to start asking questions. Once I get a lead, I'll track the man down if I have to go to hell and back."

"I wish I could go with you but I can't. I have a wild railroad and cattle town to worry about."

"I understand."

"I think we should leave and return in the morning with a buckboard for the bodies," Oatman said. "I'm not superstitious or spooky, but this place is giving me the willies. I don't want to be poking around here in the dark all night."

"We'll carry Otto into the house so that his body isn't eaten any more than it already has been."

Charlie Oatman nodded. "Let's get to it then and get the hell out of here."

"I'm with you on that," Longarm told him as he grabbed the old man's ankles. "But I'm sure not looking forward to riding Hammer back to town."

"He and Homer will be racing for the barn," Charlie said. "And as for me, I'm just going to let Homer run and put this place as far as I can from me tonight."

Longarm tried not to look at the desecrated body and not to smell the sickly sweet aura of death. And if the truth was to be known, he was as anxious as Charlie Oatman to leave this killing place.

Chapter 8

Early the next morning Longarm got up and sent a telegram to Marshal Billy Vail explaining how he and Marshal Oatman had found two dead bodies at the St. Clair Ranch and that there were no suspects in sight.

Billy replied almost immediately with a very short, terse telegram that read:

FIND AND ARREST MARSHAL LINK ST. CLAIR

Well, Longarm thought, *that's plenty clear enough.* Longarm understood that because Link St. Clair was a sworn federal officer of the law, Billy felt that the man had to be either cleared of any wrongdoing or arrested with as little public attention as possible and the sooner the better.

Longarm had some breakfast and then went to see Marshal Oatman. "Are we headed back out to the ranch soon?"

"Yeah, just as quick as Arnie can find us a buckboard and get it hitched up and ready to roll."

"He wouldn't . . ." Longarm's voice trailed off.

"Wouldn't what?" Oatman asked.

"Wouldn't hitch Homer and Hammer up to a wagon, would he?"

Despite the grimness of the job they faced this morning, Oatman managed a tired smile. "Don't worry. Arnie knows that those paint geldings would wreck a wagon and probably kill anyone driving or riding in it."

"Good," Longarm said with relief. "Have you come up with any local suspects since we got back last night?"

"Afraid not. What you said about Link makes a lot of sense."

"It does, but what a good lawman can't afford to do is to jump to conclusions and put his entire focus on what might be an innocent man."

"Are you changing your mind about Link being the most likely killer?"

"No," Longarm replied. "I still think he either killed and robbed the Chinaman . . . or knows who did."

"So we just have to find him."

"That's what I was sent up here to do and nothing has changed. Did you go to the bank yet and see if the Chinaman had a savings account?"

"He did, but not a lot," Oatman said. "So it seems likely that either most of the Chinaman's money is hidden on the ranch or it was stolen."

"What about the other man, Otto?"

"I also checked at the bank and was surprised to learn that he put most of his earnings in the bank. But that doesn't mean he didn't have cash stashed away somewhere at the ranch like the Chinaman."

"Was Otto a spender, gambler, or heavy drinker?" Longarm asked.

"He was a loner and he'd have a few beers when he came into town, but I always got the impression that he was very tight with his money. Otto was kind of a surly fella and I don't think he had many friends in Cheyenne."

"But he might have had at least a few," Longarm offered. "And when we get back with the bodies, I'll need to talk to them."

"Come to think of it, he was pretty fond of Gloria Pope."

"And who is she?"

"She's a fat and over-the-hill whore that works at a run-down hotel here in town."

"I'll talk to her as soon as we return."

"Let's go over to the livery and see if we can put the prod on Arnie. I'd like to get out there and retrieve those bodies as soon as possible. They're already plenty ripe and way overdue for burying."

Longarm thought that was the truest thing he'd heard this morning.

Longarm wasn't at all surprised to see that Arnie's buckboard was in poor shape and the horses hitched to it old, scrawny, and weak. "Charlie, is this the best that we can get for this job?"

"Oh, I'll agree that they sure don't look like much, but they'll pull the wagon to the ranch and back."

"I hope so." Now that Longarm knew that the marshal was courting Arnie's daughter, he understood that any argument on this matter would be pointless.

"It's not that far to the ranch and back," Arnie reminded them. "Just go easy on these old horses and you'll be fine."

Longarm was so annoyed that he had to bite his tongue and keep quiet as they drove out of Cheyenne.

They finally arrived at the St. Clair Ranch around noon and when they entered the house to collect the Chinaman, Longarm pulled up short.

"What's the matter!" Oatman asked with alarm.

"Someone has been here since we left last night," Longarm told the man, drawing his gun. "And they might still be around."

Oatman also unholstered his pistol and looked around. "How do you know?"

"The pantry," Longarm explained. "It was well stocked with tins when I was here last night and now it's nearly empty."

"You remember what was in the *pantry*?"

"Not exactly, but I did recall that it was full. And there was a smoked ham on the butcher-block counter that's missing. Also, it's clear that someone searched every drawer and cranny in this kitchen."

"Looking for even more food?"

"No," Longarm said, "looking for something of much greater value. Money, gold, or precious stones."

"But . . ."

"Let's search the house again," Longarm said. "And be ready just in case we're not the only ones here and for cripes' sakes don't accidently shoot me in the back if something happens fast."

"Wouldn't dream of it," the town marshal replied, trying to hide the tension in his voice.

A few minutes later it was obvious that there was no one else inside. Longarm made his way outside and quickly circled the ranch house. "Look," he said coming back around to join Oatman. "Someone was here early this morning and they tied their horse at that tree and entered by the back door."

Longarm studied fresh hoofprints leading toward the ridge and the west. "Our killer is running. He'd have known we were coming back for the bodies this morning and so he returned and found provisions and whatever else he needed to go on the run and then he took off in a helluva hurry."

"Link?"

"Only one way to find out," Longarm said. "I'll have to take one of those old wagon horses and see if there's a saddle in the barn and go after whoever was here."

"But you'd *never* catch them on either of those horses."

Longarm knew that Chief Marshal Oatman was right. Yet, it really galled him to give the killer an extra three or four hours. Still, he needed to get some supplies of his own before he set off on what could be a long and difficult manhunt.

"You're right," he said. "Let's pitch those bodies into the buckboard and make those old horses move faster going to the barn."

"Don't want to risk killing them," Oatman cautioned. "Arnie sets quite a store by those horses. Said he's had them more'n twenty years."

"I'd have guessed forty years from their appearance," Longarm said caustically. "Let's go!"

The buckboard ride back to Cheyenne was slow and tedious. Longarm tried to make the old horses walk faster but they refused. So when they finally reached Cheyenne he handed the lines over to Oatman and said, "Take 'em to the mortuary and have someone put them in the ground before sunset."

"I'll do that. What about you?"

"I'm going to find a good horse, buy some provisions and a rifle, and be on my way in two hours or less. I need to pick up that trail behind the ranch house before dark and try to make up some ground on the killer."

"Sure wish I wasn't tethered to this town," Oatman complained. "I'd like to go with you and see how you work."

"I work fast and this buckboard ride has been an agony given the time that has been wasted," Longarm told the man as he jumped off and trotted over to his hotel to get his belongings.

Ten minutes later Longarm locked his room door and headed downstairs through the lobby. "Marshal, I understand that there are two murders out at the St. Clair Ranch," the desk clerk called. "Not surprising."

Longarm stopped. "Why would you say that?"

"Something wasn't right out there. That old man that you found murdered, well, he would stay here a couple nights a month with his whore and I overheard the talk."

"What talk?"

But the desk clerk shook his head. "Just talk. I knew that Otto hated Link St. Clair and that they'd had words.

He also didn't like the Chinaman. But then, Otto didn't like anyone other than that whore."

"Whose name is Gloria Pope?"

"Yeah. Can you believe a whore would give herself the name of *the* pope!"

"Where can I find her?"

"Upstairs where you just came from," the clerk said. "She's with someone, though."

"Room number?"

"Listen, I can't . . . oh, what the hell. Room number eight."

Longarm dropped his gear and headed up the stairs. He was in a hurry, but if Gloria Pope was upstairs, then he figured he'd better take a few minutes and find out what she knew that might help him learn something valuable.

The door at room eight wasn't locked so Longarm barged inside to see a pair that were as naked as old, plucked chickens and just about as attractive. Gloria was on top and she was big with rolls of fat around her waist that were bouncing almost as violently as her huge breasts and buttocks. The man underneath her looking like he was being pounded through the mattress was small and skinny. He was still wearing his socks that had gaping holes in both toes.

"Jaysus!" Gloria shouted, twisting around to glare at Longarm. "You're gonna have to wait your damned turn outside. This isn't some gawdamn peep show, you big pervert!"

"Get off him!" Longarm yelled loud enough to get the whore's full attention. "I'm a marshal and we need to talk right now."

"Can't I at least finish him up so I won't have to do it all over again for my money?" Gloria whined. "All I need is about thirty more seconds."

The skinny man being ridden so hard wheezed, "Please, Marshal, I'm almost *there*!"

"Oh, for hell sakes," Longarm spat, whirling around and exiting the room. "You got one minute!"

A minute had almost passed when the skinny man let out a whoop and then the bedsprings went silent. Longarm, out of simple decency, gave them another couple of minutes.

"Thank you," the skinny man said, pulling on his pants as he shot out the door.

"You're welcome," Longarm replied, stepping back into the room to see Gloria lying on the bed with her big, pale thighs spread open. "Want some of this while we talk? Only cost you a dollar, Marshal."

"Hell no!" Longarm growled. "Cover yourself up, woman. I'm about to get sick to my stomach."

"Well, screw you!" she hissed, whipping the covers over her and pulling them up to her neck.

"You're Gloria Pope and you were a favorite of a man named Otto who worked at the St. Clair Ranch."

"Yeah, we like each other. I am the only friend Otto has. He wants to marry me."

"If he wants to marry you, then he must have been . . ." Longarm bit back the last of the comment.

Gloria's expression changed. "Otto must have *what*?"

"I'm sorry to have to tell you that Otto is dead."

Gloria's hand flew to her mouth. "Oh, no!"

"He and the Chinaman who worked at the ranch were murdered and I'm trying to find out who did it and why."

"That dirty, murdering bastard! I told Otto to watch out for himself."

"Who are you talking about?"

"Link St. Clair, of course! Otto hated the man and so did the Chink. They were both going to quit."

"Why would Link kill those two?"

"Money." Gloria wiped a tear from her chubby cheeks. "Otto had been saving up for years and he always told me he was going to take me out of the whorehouse and we'd go someplace far away where no one knew either of us. He was going to buy a little house and we'd live happily ever after."

"And you believed him?"

"Of course! Otto really loved me. I was saving up some money on my own and even though he was twenty-three years older than me he could still fuck like a young buck. And he was decent to me." She sobbed, entire mountain of fat shaking now. "I loved Otto. We didn't just fuck, we talked a lot and held hands, too."

"How much money had Otto saved all these years?"

"About three thousand and I have about a thousand. We figured that would take us far away and give us a good, fresh start." She dropped the sheet that had been pulled up to her neck, bent her head and began to cry.

"Gloria," Longarm said, feeling pretty rotten about what he'd been thinking about this woman, who obviously had loved a man that no one else seemed to have liked. "I'm sorry. I really am. I'm going to try to find the man that killed Otto and the Chinaman. If it's Link St. Clair, then I'll bring him to justice and that will mean a necktie party."

She looked up, sniffling. "If you find him, he'll have

Otto's money. A thousand dollars was hidden at the ranch, the rest is in the bank. It should belong to *me*."

"That won't be up to me to decide," Longarm told her. "How much do you think that the Chinaman had stashed away at the ranch?"

Gloria shrugged. "He put money in the bank, but Otto always thought he had large stashes squirreled away at the ranch."

"Do you have any idea what happened to Mrs. Lilly St. Clair?"

"No," Gloria said in a small, sad voice. "She was real nice and her husband didn't treat her right. I wouldn't be surprised if she just ran away or if Link killed her, too."

"Describe her for me please."

"What?"

"Tell me the color of her hair and her height."

Gloria did as she was asked. "That's the same woman I saw in Denver only a few days ago with a man she said was her father. Their buggy was a runaway and it overturned right in the middle of town. The old man died and then Lilly St. Clair disappeared. Any idea where she might have gone?"

Gloria Pope sniffled and blew her nose on a dirty handkerchief, then used it to wipe herself downstairs. "You know where I think she is?"

"No." Longarm had turned away for a moment, repulsed by what Gloria was doing. Now, he turned back to her and asked, "Where?"

"Underground," Gloria gravely pronounced. "That handsome bastard Link St. Clair murdered all three of them as sure as we were born."

"Do you know if he had family somewhere? Or a

friend or a place that he talked about liking? Anything you know would be of help."

Gloria leaned back on the pillow. "Otto said that he talked a lot about the gold fields in California. Said he'd been there and had struck it rich some years ago and that he always talked about going back and retrieving some gold nuggets that he'd hidden in the Sierra foothills east of Sacramento."

"Are you *sure* that's what he said?" Longarm asked.

"Yes, and Otto told me that more'n once. Said that Link was always talking about a gold town called . . . I forgot."

"Try hard to remember. If you want me to help you get that money back, then you need to remember."

"Gold Hill! That was the name of the town. She wiped her nose on the sheet. "You know, Marshal, you nearly scared the shit out of poor little Marvin just a few minutes ago."

"I didn't intend to."

"A handsome man like you ought to know when to knock."

"Sorry. Are you sure it was called Gold Hill?"

"Pretty sure." Gloria Pope began to cry so Longarm left the room in a hurry. He would sure as hell try to overtake Link before the man could rendezvous with a train that would take him through Reno and then over the Sierras to a town called Gold Hill. And if he failed to do that, he would wire Billy Vail for more money and if Billy didn't want to foot the expenses, then Longarm would just have to figure out what next to do. And at the top of his list was to find out for sure if Lilly St. Clair really was dead and buried.

Chapter 9

Longarm was stopped in the middle of the street on his way to rent a horse by the town marshal waving a telegram. "This is for you and I thought it might be important!"

Longarm quickly read the message from Billy Vail.

LILLY ST. CLAIR REAPPEARED STOP SPOKE TO ME ABOUT HER MISSING HUSBAND STOP IS ON TRAIN HEADING UP TO CHEYENNE TODAY STOP WAIT FOR HER AT DEPOT BEFORE TAKING FURTHER ACTION

"I'd say that this changes things considerably, wouldn't you?" Oatman asked.

"It does," Longarm agreed, pulling out his pocket watch. "If the train is on time, she ought to be here before long."

"Less than two hours," Oatman said.

"Then I'll wait to hear what she has to say even though it gives the killer even more of a head start."

"That killer almost certainly being Link."

"Looks that way," Longarm agreed.

"So what are you going to do now?" Oatman asked.

"I'm going to get a good meal and take a long nap. Meet Mrs. St. Clair at the station and bring her up to my room where we can all hear what she has to say about her missing husband."

"I'll do that." Oatman paused. "Gonna cost us about twenty-eight dollars to bury the Chinaman and Otto. The city is pretty tight for money right now and I was wondering if the federal . . ."

"No," Longarm said, cutting the man off. "We won't pay the twenty dollars. I'm afraid that the city fathers of Cheyenne will just have to cough up the cash."

"I was pretty sure you'd say that, but they wanted me to ask."

"Well, you did," Longarm said. "Now, I'm going to go eat and sleep."

"Between now and when the train arrives I'll keep my nose to the ground and my ears open for any useful information."

"Did Link have any close friends here in Cheyenne?"

"Sure. He was the kind of man that stood out. I don't know how many men in town actually liked him, but he got along."

"Oh, one other thing. Did Link say much to you about the train robbery?"

"Well, yeah. After it happened, that's about all that we talked about until he left town to hunt the train robbers down."

"Did he . . ." Longarm was fishing for something, but he didn't know quite what it was. "Did Link seem especially upset or agitated?"

"Hell yes! We both were." Oatman frowned. "What is it about Link that you *really* want to know?"

"Not sure," Longarm admitted. "But there is the possibility that Link was involved with the bunch that robbed the train."

"What!" Oatman cried in astonishment.

"You heard me," Longarm replied. "How much money did the gang that robbed the train get?"

"I don't know exactly. The railroad said it was over five thousand, and the gang went through the passenger cars relieving people of their money, watches, jewelry, and other valuables."

Longarm digested this information for a moment. "So that means that the gang might have pulled in as much as ten thousand."

"That's possible, I suppose."

"Lot of money. How many were in the gang?"

"There were four, according to the witnesses."

"Just four?"

"That's all. They wore hoods and canvas dusters from shoulder to toe. They were well organized and knew exactly what they were doing. For example, they held up the train while it was moving real slow on the steepest part of the uphill grade going up and over the Laramie Mountains. And they didn't say much."

"Anyone killed?"

"No," Oatman answered. "But the conductor and a couple of the porters were pistol-whipped. The four that robbed the train were making an example of them and there were no heroes that day."

"I'm sure there weren't. Was Link with you on the day that the train was robbed?"

"No, he was working out at his ranch and it was on a Sunday." Charlie Oatman toed the ground for a moment, lost in troubled thoughts. "Custis, I don't think that Link St. Clair was one of the train robbers."

"Why not?"

"He just didn't seem the type to do something like that."

"But he probably murdered his two older employees," Longarm argued. "Did Link seem like the type to do that?"

"No, sir, he did not."

"Well, there you have it," Longarm folding his arms across his chest. "Charlie, the point I'm trying to make to you is that you have to consider all the possibilities."

"I can see what you mean."

"Go back to the bank before Lilly arrives and find out if the St. Clair couple had a bank account, and if they did, was it suddenly drained of funds or does it still have a balance."

"I'll sure enough do that."

"Let me know the minute you find out," Longarm instructed. "Even if I'm asleep in my hotel room, wake me up and let me know. I want that information *before* we talk to Lilly this evening."

"Do you really think that she and her husband . . ."

"I have no earthly idea," Longarm confessed. "But if they were in financial trouble, they might have been behind not only the murders but the train robbery as well."

"I'd hope not, him being a federal marshal."

"From what I've learned so far, Link St. Clair was a

federal officer of the law in name only," Longarm said as he left the man standing in the middle of the street.

After having a big meal, Longarm retired to his room where he removed his boots and hat, then lay down and fell asleep almost immediately. When he awoke, it was dark outside and the town marshal was pounding at his door.

Longarm got up, stretched, and let the man inside. "What did you find out at the bank concerning the St. Clair couple?"

"They didn't have any money in the bank. They'd taken it all out six months ago."

"Did they withdraw a large amount . . . or just a few dollars?"

"Not much. Eighteen hundred dollars."

Longarm yawned and returned to sit on his bed. "Train should be here shortly."

"You still want me to be there when she arrives and bring her up here?"

"Yeah," Longarm said. "No use in dragging her into your office and causing a lot of tongues to wag if she's innocent of everything."

"I'm hopin' she is," Oatman said. "She always seemed like a real classy lady to me."

"I had the exact same impression."

After the town marshal was gone, Longarm cleaned himself up and combed his hair. He put on a fresh shirt and string tie, then brushed his coat and took a chair to wait.

He didn't have to wait very long. The train arrived
fifteen minutes later and Lilly was immediately escorted
up to his room.

When she saw Longarm, the color in her cheeks
drained away.

"Mrs. St. Clair, how nice to see you again," Longarm
said, offering her a chair.

Lilly's eyes jumped from one lawman to the other
and then she sighed and took a chair. Longarm decided
that she looked strained and tired, but she was still a
remarkably attractive woman.

"So," Longarm said, jumping right into it. "I understand that you went to my office and you talked to my
boss, Marshal Billy Vail."

"That's correct," Lilly replied. "But I didn't go there
to see him . . . I went there to see *you*."

"Well, here I am and here you are and let's get
started. Did my boss tell you that we found both of your
employees murdered at your ranch?"

She gulped hard and nodded.

"And did he also say that we still haven't heard from
your husband, the one you told me was dead, who sup-
posedly went off hunting for the Union Pacific train
robbers?"

Again, just the hint of a nod.

"May I call you Lilly?" Longarm asked.

"Yes."

"Are you aware of where your husband has gone?
And just as important, are you aware of *why* he has
vanished?"

"Not exactly," she whispered. "But I do know that . . .

that there may be more to this than you think, Marshal."

"Meaning?"

For the first time, she looked directly into Longarm's eyes. "Meaning it is possible that my husband murdered Li Hop and Otto Keisterman."

Longarm glanced over at Charlie Oatman, then back to Lilly. "And why would you think that?"

"Because he had become a very different person than the man I married five years ago." Lilly sighed deeply. "You see, Link was a heavy drinker even when we met. But I thought that he'd get past that as he matured. And he might have except for Li Hop."

"What could the Chinaman have done to him?" Oatman asked, leaning forward intently.

"Li Hop was a very devious man. He could cook, clean, and he was very good with numbers. After some time, we let him handle our accounts."

"And he stole from you," Longarm said.

"Yes, quite a lot of money. But even worse . . . far worse . . . he got my husband hooked on opium."

"Where the hell did he get that?" Oatman demanded.

"It comes on the eastbound train from California. There's a huge Chinatown in San Francisco, another in Sacramento. When Link lived in California as a gold seeker, he had a taste of opium and he loved it. Loved it so much he knew he had to leave and that's why he came to Colorado while he still had his right mind."

"And of course, Li Hop learned about that and used it to his advantage," Longarm concluded.

"Yes. As I said, he was devious and he knew that if

he got my husband hooked on the white powder, then he would have control of him. I didn't even know what was going on until the last."

"And that's why you left the ranch and went to Denver?"

"It is. I was running scared and I didn't know what to do. I wanted desperately for everyone to think I still had money when in fact I was penniless."

"Then how," Longarm asked in a deliberate voice, "did you happen to be in that beautiful carriage and who was the man who died when it overturned?"

"The carriage was his and he was . . . well, helping me. Mr. Danner and I weren't related, and I think he was a very kind old soul who needed someone to look after him. Albert was rich, lonely, and I knew that he wanted me."

"And that's what it was all about between you?"

"Yes."

Longarm got up and paced back and forth for a few minutes. "How about Mr. John Holt, who owns the Frontier Hotel?"

"I never met the man but knew of him through Albert. He was very kind and they were the best of friends."

"I spoke to Mr. Holt and he had no idea who you are."

"He wouldn't. With Link's craziness and what I knew would turn out to be a very bad end not only for him but for myself, I decided to change my name. One day after Albert had visited Mr. Holt at his hotel, he came back and told me that the old man had a niece who was a nun and her last name was St. Clair just like mine."

"And did you also share the same first names?"

"No. My real name is Elizabeth but I've always been called Lizzy."

Longarm had to smile. "What a coincidence. Lizzy and Lilly."

"It was easy to make the adjustment and after a short while, I actually thought of myself as Lilly. Oh, I knew that I had nowhere near the moral fiber of Mr. Holt's niece who had given her life to Christ, but I honestly tried to be a better person."

"Did you ever intend to go back to your husband and ranch?" Oatman asked.

"I . . . I didn't know if that would happen. Link had gotten very dark inside. He could still be charming when he was around others and in town, but back at the ranch he was demonized by the opium. I was afraid for my life. Once, I even confessed that to Otto."

"And what did he say?"

"Not much. I think he was also afraid of my husband. I had the feeling that he wanted very much to leave the ranch but . . . " Her voice caught but she pushed on, "Obviously, he didn't make it in time."

"So you weren't there when they were murdered?"

"Of course not. I didn't even know about it until I went to the federal office building to see you," she said, looking straight into Longarm's eyes. "And when I heard about the murders and train robbery . . . well, I just broke down and told Mr. Vail everything just as I've told both of you."

There was a long silence before Longarm said, "Do you think that your husband murdered your employees?"

"Yes, I'm afraid that I do. Li Hop was withholding the opium and demanding more and more money. He was in control. My guess is that Link murdered Li Hop and knowing that Otto would tell the authorities, he had to murder him as well."

"But you didn't see him do it."

"I just told you that I did not."

Longarm was satisfied and the explanation made good sense to him. Apparently, Chief Marshal Charlie Oatman was also satisfied.

"Lilly . . . or Lizzy, whichever you prefer . . ."

"Lilly is the better person so that is what I prefer."

Longarm dipped his chin in agreement. "Fine. The next question is important. Might your husband have robbed the Union Pacific Railroad because he was out of money and desperate for the white powder?"

"Yes. Without a doubt."

"And if he did, can you imagine who the other three accomplices might be?"

"I'd say that the most likely ones would be the Dooley brothers."

Longarm turned to the town marshal. "You know them?"

"Sure do! Rotten a family as there is in this neck of the woods. The Dooley clan are always in and out of jails and prisons. Some of them have been shot, two that I know of were hanged." He looked to Lilly. "Which of them are you talking about?"

"Ike, Quinn, and Rafe Dooley. They were thick with my husband at the last. Quinn was always trying to get to me so I never let us be alone."

"Quinn might be the worst of the three," Oatman agreed. "He's a dangerous and demented man."

Longarm gave this a moment of thought. "I'd like

to talk to those three but I can't arrest them on specu-
lation."

"They live about four miles east of Cheyenne and I'd
be willing to deputize a couple of men good with guns
and ride out there with you tomorrow," Oatman offered.
"But you'd better understand that they won't be coop-
erative and might just decide to try and kill us."

"I'll have to take that chance," Longarm said. "And
I would appreciate some support."

"Let me see if I can find some men," Oatman said.
"Won't be easy once I tell them what we're going to do.
Everyone knows about the Dooley clan and no one ever
wants to get on their bad side."

"Well," Longarm replied, "I'm going to be on their
bad side and so are you after we meet them. Are you up
to doing this, Charlie?"

The younger man nodded. "Comes with the job, I
suspect. And besides, I couldn't live with myself if I let
you go out there alone to get gunned down."

"Thanks," Longarm said, meaning it.

"Custis," Lilly said, "maybe I'm wrong about that
family. Maybe I'm wrong in thinking that my husband
was part of the holdup gang. It might be someone else
entirely and I don't want you killed because . . ."

Longarm held up his hand to silence her. "I appreciate your concern, but I wear a badge and a train was
robbed. It's my job and also that of Charlie here to pur-
sue this and find the robbers as well as the killers of Li
Hop and Otto Keisterman."

"I know, but . . ."

"Just get a room and try to rest," Longarm advised
the woman. "Charlie and I will be back tomorrow and

perhaps by then we'll have a lot more answers than questions."

"All right," she said. "I'll see if they have any rooms here. But before I leave here I want you to know that I had nothing to do with those murders or the train robbery. And I am very sorry for the lies I told you when we met in Denver."

"Apology accepted," Longarm told her. "Now, good night."

They left and Longarm lay back down on his bed. So *many* questions! Was Lilly or Lizzy St. Clair really her name or was that all just another lie? Did her husband murder the Chinaman and Otto for their money and perhaps a big cache of opium? And had Lilly and her husband once been in love with honestly earned money or had they lied and cheated someone out of it perhaps even back in California?

Longarm had purchased a bottle of good whiskey that morning, and because his head was about to explode with all those troubling questions he poured himself a drink and dragged a chair over to the window so he could look down on the street and watch normal people doing normal things. And maybe he could just drown a few of the sharper images from his mind of Li Hop and Otto Keisterman's decomposing bodies.

Chapter 10

It was well after midnight when Longarm was awakened by a knock at his door. He figured it was just some drunk who had forgotten his room number. "Go away!"

"It's *me*," she whispered.

Longarm sat up and shook his head. "Who? Is that you, Gloria? If it is, then leave me to my sleep."

"It's . . . it's Lilly!" she hissed from out in the hallway.

Longarm wasn't wearing a stitch of underwear so he hauled on his pants and went to the door. He opened it a crack and sure enough, it really was Lilly St. Clair. "What do you want at this hour?"

"I can't sleep. I'm worried that you and Charlie are going to get shot up and maybe worse. I . . . I feel completely responsible."

"Come on in if you need to talk a minute or two," Longarm said, stifling a yawn. "But, Lilly, I wear a badge and so does Charlie, so even if you had nothing

to do with all this, we'd still be going out there to the
Dooley place tomorrow."

"I know," she said, slipping inside his room and clos-
ing the door behind her. "But even so, I was afraid that
I might finally fall asleep just before dawn and you and
the marshal would already have left. Then, if things go
wrong you'd both be dead and I'd . . ."

Lilly bent her head and began to cry.

"Oh, for hell sakes, Lilly," Longarm said, wrapping
an arm over her shoulders and leading her to a chair.

"It's just that I've seen so much go wrong in the last
few months and even before that being around Link
when he was smoking opium was like living with the
devil himself. And then Albert dying in that wreck we
had and now this. I feel like I'm going to explode into
a million tiny pieces that can never be put back together
again!"

"How about a big shot of good whiskey? That might
help."

"I'm not much of a drinker, Custis. And I didn't come
here to make advances, either. I just wanted to tell you
that I've made a complete mess of my life and I'm very
sorry that you and that town marshal may have to face
the consequences of those mistakes."

Longarm found a second glass and poured them both
a couple of fingers of whiskey. "Drink this and you'll
feel better."

"But worse tomorrow."

"Maybe so, but I thought you said you needed some
help tonight. Tomorrow the sun will rise and shine and
the world will look a whole lot more cheerful."

"Not if the Dooley clan kills you and the marshal. If that happens, I'll probably slit my wrists, curl up, and die."

Longarm hoped that was an attempt at humor, but he wasn't sure. He reached out and lifted Lilly's hands with her drink right up to her lips. "Drink," he ordered, reaching for his own glass.

So they both drank and then Longarm sat down on his bed and studied Lilly in the moonlight that flowed through his open window. "May I ask how old you are, Lilly?"

"Thirty-two going on eighty-two."

"You're a beautiful woman and I suspect a good one who made some bad choices."

"I always did when it came to men."

"Well," Longarm said with a chuckle, "I'm not too good when it comes to choosing women, either."

"Oh, really?" She managed a smile and took another drink. "How bad are you?"

"I'm terrible," he confessed. "I pass by the good ones if they're not pleasing to my eye and I grab hold of the bad ones more than I should."

"I'm not a 'bad one,' Custis. But right now, I feel as if I've screwed up my life so thoroughly that I can never get it back on track."

"Are you penniless?"

"Quite the contrary," she said. "The ranch is paid off because I fought Link for years when he tried to borrow on it for more opium. And before he died, dear, sweet Albert gave me a diamond ring and necklace that are worth thousands of dollars."

"Did you . . ."

"No," she said, "I didn't sleep with him or even go after his money. At least not any more than he went after my looks and youth. But Albert was alone and he liked to give me things. I was afraid that Link would find and kill me and I was trying to figure out what to do when that carriage overturned and my dear friend Albert died."

"Why did you disappear the next day when I went to see you?"

"I was afraid. You'd told me that you were a lawman and I'd lied to you and knew you'd eventually learn the truth. I needed some time to think things out and when I finally decided that I had to unburden my conscience, I went to see you at the Federal Building fully prepared to make a confession."

"And in the hope that I might become your protector if your crazy husband showed up in Denver."

"Yes," Lilly admitted. "I freely admit that there was that element of self-protection in my thinking. But now, Link is missing and people are dead. If I'd have told you about him, perhaps Li Hop and Otto would still be alive."

"They were murdered before we met," Longarm said flatly.

Her eyes widened with shock. "They were?"

"Yes. When we found them their bodies were in bad shape. That's why I told the marshal here to get them buried right away."

"Oh." She took another drink. "Thank you for telling me that. At least that is no longer on my conscience."

Longarm finished his drink. "Lilly, I need to get a decent night's sleep if I'm going to be at my best tomorrow. If I'm not and something goes amiss and Charlie is killed, I'd never forgive myself."

"I need sleep, too. Do you mind if I join you?"

"Hell no," he said, unbuckling his belt and dropping his pants to climb back into bed. "It's your choice."

"I'll take my chances for the rest of this long, depressing night that you are honorable and a gentleman."

Lilly removed all but her underclothes and climbed into bed with Longarm. He rubbed her back for a moment thinking that, for the first time that he could remember, he was going to bed with a beautiful woman and doing nothing but getting some much-needed sleep.

Morning came all too quickly and Longarm left Lilly St. Clair sleeping like a baby. He had a light breakfast and then headed up the street to the marshal's office. Charlie Oatman was cleaning a double-barreled shotgun and he looked like he'd not slept in days.

"You need a rifle to borrow?" Charlie asked.

"Shotgun like that would be about right."

"I've got another."

"Are you the only lawman on the town's payroll?" Longarm asked.

"I had a deputy but some track layers beat him up so badly one night in a saloon that he nearly died. When he did get well enough to walk, he took the train out of town. I heard he settled in Laramie and is working as a typesetter. He was too nice and trusting to be a lawman. I've thought it out and realize that he was lucky he didn't get killed during the short time I had him on the town's payroll."

"You really need help here," Longarm said.

"That's sort of what I thought I had when Link St. Clair arrived. He said he was sent here to do some work for the railroad but he never would talk about it."

"He worked *for* the railroad?" Longarm asked.

"No, he was trying to solve a few previous holdups. I'm not sure if they paid him some money besides his federal income."

"Then he knew things about the railroad and that would help him hold it up when he needed the opium money."

"I guess so," Charlie answered, looking completely distracted. "Have you had any breakfast?"

"As a matter of fact I have."

"I tried to eat this morning but my stomach won't hold a thing except coffee. I've drunk a gallon or more and now my nerves are strung tighter than fiddle strings."

"What about finding a few men to go with us?" Longarm asked.

"I've lined up three good men. They should be here at any time."

"I don't want any hotheads," Longarm warned. "We need solid, levelheaded boys that will follow my orders."

"I think these three will," Charlie promised just as the door to his office crashed open.

Three disheveled and obviously stinking-drunk cowboys stood grinning in the doorway for a moment until one bellowed, "Marshal, how much did you say that you were gonna pay us each if we live through this day?"

"Twenty dollars each," Charlie told them.

The cowboy grabbed hold of the door to steady

himself. "I expect that to face the Dooley people we'll need a lot more pay than that, Marshal. We'll be puttin' our lives right on the line."

"No, you won't be," Longarm shot back. "You won't be putting your lives anywhere near us. Go sleep it off, all of you."

The cowboys swayed in the doorway and studied Longarm. Finally, their spokesman said, "Hell, we're up for this for fifty dollars each!"

"Get out of my sight before you land in this jail."

The men recoiled and then they turned and staggered off shouting oaths at Longarm and Charlie.

"So much for the backup," Longarm drawled.

"I know those three and they're not usually like that," Charlie said, biting a hangnail. "I thought they'd be pretty sober this morning and they all are handy with six-guns."

"They are not what we need," Longarm said with an edge in his voice.

"Maybe I could round up a few others?" Charlie hopefully suggested. "It sure would help to ride out to the Dooley place in force."

"I expect that it would," Longarm agreed. "But that could also backfire on us if they thought we'd come to make war. With just the two of us they won't be too worried and we might be able to make more headway."

"That's one hell of an optimistic point of view," Charlie grumbled. "One that very well might get us riddled with bullets and buckshot."

Longarm grabbed Charlie's shotgun and inspected it. "One of these can be a great equalizer," he told the junior lawman. "You said you have another."

"I do."

"Then get it and be ready to use the damned thing," Longarm ordered. "And don't tell me that we're going to have to rent Arnie's two paint giraffes again."

Oatman turned away, unable to meet his eyes. "Sorry, Custis."

"Shit," Longarm grated. "Well, at least if they take off running from us, we know we can overtake them."

"The Dooley men aren't the kind that will run."

"I've heard that too many times when it wasn't true," Longarm shot back. "One thing you'd better understand, Charlie. If it comes down to slinging lead, I'll be the first man to do 'er and the last one standing."

Chief Marshal Charlie Oatman nodded and lifted his chin. "Let's get this over with."

"My thoughts exactly," Longarm replied.

They were about ready to climb on the stomping and snorting Hammer and Homer when Lilly rushed up to them and threw her arms first around Charlie and then around Longarm. "I pray that this will work out and you will both return safely."

"Thanks," Charlie said. "But if it don't, go see my sweetheart and tell her I loved her."

"Who is she?"

"Arnie's daughter."

Lilly couldn't hide her disbelief. "That ugly man with one leg has a daughter that *you* love?"

"Sure do."

"Then I'll go see her right away and . . ."

"No," Charlie objected. "She's a mess since I told her

what we were going to do today. I think she'd do better if you just left her alone."

"That's because you don't know anything about women," Lilly retorted. "I'll console her. After all, I've got my heart in this, too."

Longarm's eyebrows lifted in a question. "What does *that* mean?"

"You slept with me and you don't know?"

Charlie Oatman almost dropped his teeth when he heard Lilly say that and Longarm felt his own cheeks warm. "Well, hell, Lilly, why don't you just tell everyone in Cheyenne our secret?"

"Custis, I wanted Charlie to know and I'll want his girl to know that if things go terribly wrong and you don't return why I'll be grieving."

"Wish you hadn't told me that, Lilly."

Longarm swung a leg over the top of Hammer and gawdamn if the jug-headed paint didn't bolt out of the livery yard running like his ass was ablaze!

Maybe that was just as well. Homer would soon catch up and they'd make a record-breaking streak to the Dooley place and get this over with before noon.

"Come on, Charlie!" Longarm shouted, looking over his shoulder at the younger lawman whose horse was stretched out and running like its ass was also on fire. "I don't even know which damned direction we're supposed to be goin'!"

Charlie shouted something back but Longarm couldn't make out his words. Not that it really mattered for the next mile or two.

Chapter 11

"There it is," Charlie said, pointing straight into the distance. "How should we play this?"

"We'll just ride in and keep a sharp eye out for an ambusher." Longarm shifted the shotgun so that it rested across his saddle just behind the horn. "Watch their stance. If they put their feet apart and stiffen, you know they're going to go for their guns. But whatever you do, Charlie, wait until I've gotten in close and given them both barrels."

"I don't think they'll want to fight until they find out our intentions."

"I sure hope not," Longarm replied. "But if they do open fire, we'll need to take cover as fast as we can." Longarm nodded toward a barn, sheds, and some corrals. "That's about the closest we can reach."

"Understood."

"Look," Charlie said, "they've already spotted us coming."

Longarm watched three large, barking dogs coming at them full tilt. "Hope they don't bite these horses and spook 'em up. The last thing we need is to get bucked out here on open ground."

"You got that right," Charlie replied, tightening his reins and grabbing onto his saddle horn.

"Damnation!" Longarm swore as Hammer took the bit in his mouth, laid back his ears and charged forward. Longarm was powerless to stop the runaway pinto as it scattered the dogs and then whirled around in an attempt to stomp them into the ground.

Longarm lost his seat and nearly toppled to the ground. The shotgun went flying and it was all that he could do to keep from being pitched into the sky by Hammer. Cussing and fuming, he drew his pistol, righted himself in the saddle and fired at the dogs in a desperate attempt to drive them back toward the ranch.

Unfortunately, his errant bullet creased the hip of the largest dog. The beast yelped in pain, turned tail and raced back toward the ranch. When the other two mongrels saw their leader in retreat, they skidded to a halt and reversed directions racing for the Dooley men standing in front of their ranch house.

"Jaysus!" Charlie shouted, finally getting control over Homer, "this sure isn't starting out well."

Longarm was beyond furious at his big jug-headed pinto. He yanked so hard on the reins that the animal's massive head shot straight up, nostrils flaring at the sky and then Longarm plow-reined it around in a circle, booting Hammer viciously in the ribs.

Longarm and Charlie finally managed to get both

rented geldings under control while the Dooley men howled with derisive laughter.

"I feel like a complete fool," Charlie hissed.

"Don't let this little ruckus rattle you," Longarm grated as he righted himself in the saddle and considered shooting Hammer in the head. "Just steady up and act like nothing just happened."

"Maybe we should turn around and come back tomorrow," the town marshal suggested.

But Longarm could see the Dooley men weren't laughing anymore and they looked like they were ready for a fight. He watched them exchange words and then step a few feet apart with their hands dropping toward their six-guns.

They've decided that this isn't a friendly visit, Longarm thought to himself.

"That's far enough," the oldest of the four shouted through a face-full of white whiskers. "State your business, Marshal Oatman!"

"We come to talk about Link St. Clair and the train robbery."

"Me and my boys got nothing to say about him or no robbery!"

"I think you do," Oatman said, casting a nervous side-glance at Longarm. "We came on official business and I mean to have some words with you and your boys."

"I'll tell you one more time. We've got nothin' to say to you or that big son of a bitch you rode in with, Charlie. Turn your ugly pinto horses around and haul ass off my ranch while you still can!"

"Can't do that, Elliot. I need some answers and I think you have 'em."

Longarm had seen plenty of hard, dangerous men in his life, and he knew that when Elliot Dooley pulled his pistol the old bastard would be shooting to kill just like his three sons. Even worse, he'd dropped his shotgun and Charlie's shotgun wouldn't be of much use at this range.

"Let's ride out of here!" Longarm yelled, pulling his Colt gun and snapping off a shot as the old man and his three sons drew their weapons and began firing.

Marshal Charlie Oatman paused just a moment to unleash a huge blast with both barrels of his scattergun. Smoke roiled and Longarm glanced over his shoulder to see that the shotgun's lead had actually struck several of the Dooley men, who were twitching and rolling across the dirt.

"Make for that barn!" Longarm shouted, booting his horse and sending it flying toward the open barn door. He looked back and saw that Charlie was slumped over in his saddle, bloodstain already blossoming across his shirt.

"Come on, Charlie!" Longarm yelled as Hammer raced into the barn, then skidded to a halt again, almost pitching Longarm over its big head.

"I'm hit!" Charlie yelled, tumbling from his saddle and landing heavily somewhere in the dark interior of the barn.

Longarm ran almost blindly to the marshal's side as their horses bolted back out the barn door and galloped toward Cheyenne. He glanced around and saw old man Dooley and his bleeding sons advancing with their guns blazing.

The nearly dark interior of the barn had stalls lined along its back wall, a buckboard missing a wheel and a low hayloft that covered half its floor. Otherwise, it was empty except for some harnesses, tools, and various odds and ends.

"Charlie, how bad are you wounded?"

"Bad," Charlie whispered, his voice ragged and faint. "You'd better try and save yourself."

With his eyes not yet accustomed to the darkness, Longarm groped and probed at the wounded man, trying to learn how much blood he was losing. Charlie's shirtfront was slick with warm blood, telling Longarm the Cheyenne lawman was in desperate shape.

"I'm going to die," Charlie moaned. "Reload my shotgun."

"I have no idea where it is," Longarm answered. "And you're not going to die and I'm not going *anywhere*."

"Then you'd better put them all down," Charlie whispered. "Because that's what they aim to do to us."

"Just . . . just hang on while I try to kill 'em."

"You'd better," Charlie groaned.

Longarm made his way toward the barn doors. He saw old man Dooley and his sons moving cautiously across the yard with their raised guns. When they caught a glimpse of Longarm's shadowy figure, they opened fire.

Longarm threw his shoulder to the insides of the barn doors, praying that the bullets didn't find him as splinters tore through the air. Doors finally closed, he grabbed a heavy keg of old horseshoes and rolled it up against the doors, then fumbled his way back to the wounded marshal. Thin shafts of light lanced through the barn from outside, but it was still almost as dark as a dungeon.

"Charlie, where are you hit?" Longarm asked, dragging the man toward the momentary safety offered by a stall.

"In my guts and right leg," Charlie moaned.

Longarm heard the Dooley men slamming their bodies up against the barn's heavy double doors, trying to shove them open. "Charlie, I can't help you right now. Just try and hold on for a few minutes."

"Custis, we're trapped! They'll kill us for sure."

"Not if I kill them first."

Longarm's eyes were finally beginning to adjust to the bad light. He suddenly made out the dark image of Charlie's shotgun. Snatching it up, he hissed, "Give me a couple of shells for the scattergun!"

"They're . . . they're in my vest pocket," Charlie whispered, voice fading.

Longarm found the shells, extracted the empties, and reloaded the shotgun. "Stay down and keep quiet," he ordered, spotting a ladder leading up to the loft as the barn doors began to open inch by inch.

Longarm sprinted to the ladder and went up it fast. He dropped on his stomach in grass hay and shoved the shotgun into the open air just as the barn doors burst open.

The four Dooley men were bold and stupid with rage and bloodlust. For just a fraction of a second they were silhouetted against the bright light of day, and that was when Longarm pulled both barrels down and delivered a murderous volley of thunder from on high.

For an instant, the smoke from his shotgun obliterated the view, but when it cleared Longarm saw the terrible and bloody carnage that he'd wrought. All of the Dooley men were flopping around on the dirt floor. Old man Dooley's beard and the lower half of his face was completely missing while one of his son's arm and shoulder were splattered grotesquely across the half-opened barn door.

"Please, help!"

Two Dooley brothers were still alive, but barely, and when Longarm dropped his empty shotgun in the sweet-smelling loft hay and drew his Colt revolver, he showed them no mercy and they stopped wailing forever.

Longarm holstered his pistol and climbed back down to the barn floor. "Charlie?"

"Yeah?"

"I'm getting you out of here," Longarm vowed, moving toward the man and then gently picking him up and carrying him outside.

An old woman with a rifle was standing half way between the barn and the ranch house. The three huge dogs were crowded around her barking and clearly scared witless. Longarm had been focused on the badly wounded marshal in his arms, but now the dogs made his head snap up.

"You son of a bitch!" the old woman screamed, sighting down the barrel of her rifle. "You killed all of my menfolk!"

Longarm froze, helpless with the wounded lawman a deadweight in his arms. There was no chance to reach down and grab his empty pistol, no chance to turn and run for cover.

The old woman fired from a distance of less than

thirty feet. Longarm felt Charlie Outman's body jerk in his arms when the rifle slug punched the lawman in his side. The old woman wailed an unearthly sound and began to lever another shell into the chamber of her Winchester. Longarm dropped and fell behind the man he was carrying and he tore Charlie's pistol from his holster.

They both fired at almost the same instant. The old crone was a decent shot but Longarm was an *expert* shot. His bullet struck the old lady Dooley dead center in her scrawny, skin-wattled neck and pierced her jugular vein, then her spine. Blood spurted like a fountain, and she toppled over backward with her heels kicking at the hard dirt and her thin mouth moving silently with dying curses.

Longarm turned to his friend. "Charlie?"

But Charlie Oatman was dead.

Longarm climbed to his feet, shook off dirt, and looked over his shoulder at the death trap of a barn. He turned and slowly walked over to the woman, whose scrawny body yet trembled in the final throes of death. The three big mongrels were standing over her now, growling at Longarm but at the same time shivering with fear as Longarm reloaded his Colt.

"Damn," Longarm whispered to himself as he hung his head.

He stood like that for several minutes, listening to the ranch dogs growl and blaming himself for allowing a very good man like Chief Marshal Charlie Oatman to die.

Where had it all gone so wrong? *The jug-headed giraffes.* They'd bolted when the dogs charged them and after that everything had been a crazy blood storm.

For just a fleeting moment, Longarm vowed that when he finally got back to Cheyenne he would walk up to those pintos and shoot them dead. But that moment passed and he knew that the ugly pintos were no more responsible for the outcome of this fight than were the three mongrels still trying to put up a show of bravery.

Longarm skirted the cowering, growling dogs and the dead woman and went up to the house. He figured he'd find some whiskey inside and he suddenly was dying for a drink and silent time to put his mind back in a healthy place.

So much blood. So much death.

And such a waste because with all the Dooley clan dead, he still didn't have the slightest idea where he might find Link St. Clair or if the man was even involved in the train robbery whose casualties now lay in the stillness of death all around him.

Chapter 12

Longarm stepped into the ramshackle Dooley ranch house and the smell was overpowering and instantly revolting. The big front room was a pigpen with rotting food on tin plates scattered here and there and old, unwashed clothes tossed into stinking piles. What little furniture there was looked like it had been dragged at the end of a rope through hell and back. There were cigarette butts ground out on the rough plank floors, saddles and other gear in various stages of repair and a big cast-iron stove in one corner whose stovepipe was busted.

Longarm saw some doors and figured he would hunt for the kitchen, which would be the most likely place to find whiskey. The first door he passed through was a narrow hallway lined with four open doorways to bedrooms. Longarm tried another door and found the kitchen more by following his nose than using his vision.

The kitchen was a wreck with more rotting food and a side of bloody beef hanging on meat hook near the back window. Flies buzzed over the still freshly butchered beef and there were knives and a sharpening stone lying on a rough kitchen counter.

"Where the hell is their whiskey?" he asked impatiently as he began to search the room. At the same time he was hoping to come upon some evidence tying this bunch to the train robbery.

Longarm found a jug and pulled the cork. The whiskey was better than expected. It burned like fire down his gullet and hit his stomach like a red-hot poker. Longarm took a second pull on the jug. His mind forced itself away from all the killing and he began to think of what he would do next. Find a couple of horses. There had to be a few somewhere close and then he'd see if there was a buckboard or wagon that wasn't all busted up and able to carry the bodies back to Cheyenne. It would be damned hard to face the townsfolk there and tell them that their popular young marshal was dead. And what was the name of the girl Charlie Oatman had been sparking? Longarm just couldn't remember right at the moment but knew her name would come to him soon enough.

How could he explain why he alone had survived while four Dooley men lay dead along with the marshal of Cheyenne?

Longarm knew that he'd just tell them all the truth and let the chips fall where they might. He didn't need to stay in Cheyenne, not even for the burial of Charlie Oatman . . . but he would out of duty and respect.

Longarm raised the jug to his broad shoulder and took another deep drink and then he slammed the jug down on the counter, placed both hands on it, and hung his head.

Suddenly and without warning, a crazy-eyed young Indian woman jumped out from a pantry with a butcher knife, screeching, "Aiieeeee!"

Longarm spun and threw up his forearm to block her knife thrust, but he just wasn't quick enough and the woman buried the blade deep into his shoulder. He staggered backward, tripping over a sack of beans and sprawled across the floor. The wild woman threw herself on him and plunged her big knife at his face. Longarm twisted and the tip of the blade punched into the plank flooring.

The Indian woman was dirty and incredibly strong. She screamed in frustration as she struggled to pull her knife free. Longarm had just enough strength to buck the woman aside. He tore his Colt from its holster as the woman freed her knife and slashed his arm. The gun spun away and when the Indian tried to bury her blade in his chest, Longarm kicked her in the stomach hard enough to knock her over backward.

She screamed again and hurled the knife at him but missed. Longarm took aim but held his fire as she scrambled out of the kitchen and went running toward the front door to disappear in the yard.

Longarm heard her fading cries filled with a terror that he could hope he would never experience. He wanted to catch and calm her, talk to her, and try to understand why she had attacked, but he was weak and bleeding profusely.

Longarm grabbed a table and pulled himself erect. Head swimming, he lurched over to a counter where he found a dirty towel, which he used to staunch the flow of blood.

For a minute, he swayed unsteadily on his feet, trying to summon the will to get out of this house and breathe some fresh, invigorating air. He knew that he needed a doctor's attention and that the nearest one was in Cheyenne. Taking deep breaths and trying to stop his head from spinning, Longarm thought that maybe he could find a horse and . . .

Suddenly, his knees buckled and Longarm felt himself falling toward the filthy kitchen floor.

"Custis!"

Lilly was kneeling beside him, slapping his face and shaking his head from side to side. "Custis, please don't die on me!"

Her voice sounded as if it was coming from the inky depths of a Comstock Lode mine.

"How . . . how did you know to come and find me?" he managed to ask.

"Those big pinto geldings came racing through town and ran straight into their corral at the livery. Arnie came and found me at the hotel and we knew that something had gone terribly wrong out here at the Dooley place. He gave me a horse and said he'd hitch up a wagon and come along as soon as possible."

"I hope it's a big enough wagon to carry us and four corpses," Longarm told her.

"What happened?" Lilly asked.

"Old man Dooley and his three sons weren't interested in talking," Longarm replied. "They came at us with guns blazing."

"I saw Marshal Oatman laying dead out in the yard along with the Dooley men."

"It was a bad fight," Longarm confessed. "I was hoping we could maneuver in close and get the drop on them, but they knew we'd come to arrest them."

"What a shame that the marshal died."

"Yeah."

Lilly touched his shoulder. "And this wound of yours . . ."

"There's an Indian woman somewhere around here and she's either crazy or frightened out of her mind. I was doing a search when she came at me so fast with a knife that there was no chance to protect myself."

"Where did she go?"

"I've no idea," Longarm said. "If I had to guess, she was in her twenties and was either a full-blood or a half-breed captive being held here to pleasure the Dooley brothers. And maybe even the old man."

Lilly shuddered. "Did the woman say anything?"

"No, she just screamed and attacked before she ran out of this room. I'm not sure if she was in her right mind." Longarm grimaced and tried to stand. "Lilly, can you help me out of this house?"

"Of course."

With Lilly's help, Longarm was able to make his way outside. He studied the dead and it reminded him of something he'd seen once during a raid when he'd fought in the Civil War. Flies were already buzzing around the bodies and the three mongrels would soon be eating their former masters.

"We've got to get those bodies covered and then moved and buried," he said.

Lilly avoided looking at all the dead. "I sure hope that Arnie will be here soon."

"Me, too," Longarm said, sitting heavily on a stump near the barn.

"Look!" Lilly cried, pointing with excitement.

Longarm followed her eyes toward a thick stand of pines but he didn't see a thing. "What?"

"I saw her! I saw the Indian woman who stabbed you."

Longarm studied the trees and still didn't see anything. "She might have a rifle and if that's the case, we'd better go into the barn. That woman is probably crazy enough to kill us both."

But Lilly shook her head as the Indian woman stepped out into open view. She wasn't armed and there wasn't a knife in her hands. She was moving toward them walking very slowly. Now that she was in the full light of day Longarm could see that she was either a half-breed or a Mexican woman. She was slender and dark with long and tangled black hair. Her clothes were nothing but rags and from the look of her face, she'd recently been severely beaten.

"I'm going to meet her," Lilly decided.

"Be careful. She might have another knife hidden in her dress."

"I don't think so," Lilly decided. "She looks a lot more scared than angry or crazy."

Longarm reached down and unholstered his gun, then laid it across his lap. If the woman was crazy and did have a knife intending to kill Lilly and then himself, he was going to put a bullet through her demented brain.

Chapter 13

Lilly St. Clair was not fainthearted, but as she slowly walked out to meet the dark-skinned woman she thought her knees were knocking. They stopped about ten feet apart and Lilly felt a sudden wash of pity as she studied this small person who was so frail and abused. Her hair was tangled and matted, her face swollen, and one eye was swollen half shut.

Lilly took a deep breath. "Do you speak English?"

"Some," the woman whispered.

"What is your name?"

She raised her head and for the first time looked Lilly straight in the eye. "Nolita."

"My name is Lilly." She pointed back toward the ranch house without turning because she did not expose herself to a sudden attack. "Do you live here?"

"I lived in Nevada." Nolita pointed to the west, then her expression grew dark and sad. "Now, I am here."

"Did you . . ." Lilly was not sure how exactly to ask her next question but it did need to be asked. "Were you married to one of those Dooley men?"

The corners of Nolita's split lips turned downward in contempt. "I was sold by a scalp hunter from Nevada who brought me to these men, who kept me here for their pleasure."

"I'm sorry," Lilly said, shaking her head and feeling her own anger building. "How long have they kept you here?"

"Long time. Maybe two years."

"Oh, my God," Lilly said quietly. "Didn't you ever try to run away?"

"Many times. They always catch, then beat me."

Lilly didn't quite know what to say to that. "Do you want to go back to Nevada?"

"I am Paiute," Nolita explained. "My wickiup is far away. My family all dead. Only two brothers maybe still alive. I want to see them or sit by their graves to sing and cry."

"I will help you do that," Lilly said without hesitation. "We will help you find out if your brothers are alive."

But instead of looking happy, Nolita shook her head. "Too far away. I . . . I am soiled *whore* now."

"No!" Lilly lowered her voice not wanting to frighten the woman any more than she already appeared to be. "You are *not* a whore, Nolita. You were a slave. Bought and sold by an evil man to other evil men. No one needs to know what you have suffered here."

"Nolita never forget."

Lilly stepped forward until she was face-to-face with the poor wretch. "I will help you. That man I am with is a federal marshal and his name is Custis Long. I'm sure that he will also help you."

Nolita's smile was nothing less than chilling when she stepped to one side and pointed toward the dead Dooley men. "He kill all those?"

"Yes."

"Sorry I stabbed him so bad."

"You didn't know," Lilly told her. "You didn't know that he was a good man and that he would not have harmed you."

Nolita gestured back toward the ranch house. "I go inside and find medicines now." She pointed at Charlie Oatman's body. "Who that other dead man?"

Lilly followed her eyes. "He was also good."

"I sorry he dead then."

"Me, too," Lilly said, reaching out with her hand.

Nolita hesitated for a moment, then seemed to come to some momentous decision. She reached out and touched fingers with Lilly and then she turned and walked slowly back into the ranch house.

Lilly returned to sit beside Longarm who asked, "What did she have to say about stabbing me?"

"She said she was sorry and thought you were bad like all the other white men she has known."

"She almost killed me and all she could say was that she was sorry she made a mistake?"

"You don't understand," Lilly said patiently. "That woman is Paiute and her name is Nolita. She was taken from her people and maybe her parents were murdered at the time. She says she might have two living brothers but she is too ashamed to go to find them because in her eyes she is a whore unworthy of any love or forgiveness."

"Don't know about the 'whore' part of her, but I'm not sure that I can forgive Nolita for planting a butcher knife about four inches deep into my shoulder."

"Try hard," Lilly urged. "She deserves some sympathy and understanding. You and I can't even begin to imagine what hell she has been through here at this ranch."

"Okay," Longarm grudgingly agreed. "But before I turn my back on that woman I'm going to make damned sure she isn't carrying another knife."

"*I'll* make sure," Lilly told him. "She's already had enough of the white man's touch to last her a lifetime."

Longarm studied Lilly and then he nodded his head with understanding.

When Arnie arrived he brought a topless Conestoga wagon pulled by four mules. Maybe he thought that he would be able collect something valuable from the Dooley Ranch for himself or perhaps he just anticipated a bloodbath. Either way the big overland wagon was plenty large enough. With his bad shoulder and not wanting to risk having the wound reopen, Longarm wasn't of much help in lifting and carrying the bodies of the dead and heaving them up into the wagon. And Arnie wasn't a bit happy when Longarm refused to let him also load some halfway serviceable saddles and harnesses into the wagon to keep for himself.

"Gawdamnit," Arnie swore. "Whose gonna pay me for comin' all the way out here and then bustin' my ass handlin' dead men? Huh? Who is gonna pay me for my time, wagon, and these mules?"

Longarm was in no shape to fight with the ornery old

skinflint so he allowed him to take three saddles, a complete set of harnesses, an anvil, and some horseshoeing supplies.

"I'll just sit in the back with these corpses," Longarm said, climbing into the back of the Conestoga. "Arnie, the ladies can sit up front with you."

"I don't want to sit near that stinkin' whore!"

If Longarm had been able to he would have knocked the old bastard to his knees, but instead Lilly did him one better. "Arnie," she said, voice trembling with anger, "this woman was a captive slave! She didn't come here of her own free will and that means she isn't a whore. You call her that again here or in town and I'll personally shoot your balls off!"

Arnie blanched and huffed with indignation, but he didn't say another word when he climbed up on the wagon's seat and then drove them back to Cheyenne.

It would have been hard to understate the effect that they had on the townsfolk of Cheyenne when they drove up the main street and stopped in front of the mortuary. Longarm supposed that word had gotten out that he and Charlie Oatman were going to the Dooley Ranch and that nothing good would come out of that visit. But when the people gathered around the back of the big wagon and saw Longarm with his bloody shoulder sitting next to five dead men including their town marshal, they were stunned.

"What in God's name happened out there!" a self-important man that Longarm remembered owned a mercantile store demanded. "Good heavens, it looks like a damned massacre!"

"I'll talk to everyone later," Longarm snapped.

"Meanwhile you and some of these other rubberneckers need to grab a hold of the dead and get them inside the mortuary."

"I'm not touching those bodies!" the man cried, backing up quickly.

Longarm was filled with disgust. "Chief Marshal Charlie Oatman was a good man who died trying to bring some justice! Now you people step forward like men and do what I tell you, by gawd, or there will be hell to pay!"

To emphasize his point, Longarm drew his Colt and pointed it over their heads. Not surprisingly, the mercantile owner and the others did his bidding.

An hour later after being seen and attended to by the town's best doctor, Longarm stood on the boardwalk and addressed an anxious crowd. He told them what had happened at the Dooley Ranch and how their marshal had fought bravely but had been killed. They wanted to know all the details but Longarm wouldn't give them that much time.

"Well, what are we supposed to do about a new town marshal?" someone demanded.

"Find some good candidates and offer to pay them more than you paid Oatman. Then, let them make their speeches and vote yourselves a winner," Longarm said simply.

"And whose gonna shoulder the cost of burying five men!"

"Hell if I know," Longarm said, biting back his anger. "Just give Marshal Oatman's body the respect that it deserves. As for the Dooley men, you can toss them in your shitters and burn the crappers down over their heads for all I care."

"That's the best damned idea I heard in years!" a woman standing in the back of the crowd yelled causing some to laugh. "Those Dooley men were born to be hanged and I mean that about every last one of them!"

"So do what you want with their bodies," Longarm said.

"Who is the dirty squaw!" a man shouted.

Longarm turned to Nolita for a moment and saw her cringing in shame. He twisted around toward the man who had yelled the question and said, "She was a slave to the Dooley men and if you call her a whore again, I'll by gawd put a boot up your sorry ass so deep you will be walking on your toes!"

After that, no more was said and Longarm, accompanied by the beautiful Lilly St. Clair and the pathetic Paiute woman, went to the hotel intent on not coming back out in public for as long as they could help it.

Chapter 14

Longarm sent a telegram to Marshal Billy Vail in Denver explaining what had happened so far in Cheyenne and how he'd been stabbed the day before but expected a full recovery. He also told him that the marshal of Cheyenne had been shot and killed and that he suspected that Link St. Clair was behind the train robbery.

That evening, a terse reply was received from Billy Vail that read:

GO AFTER LINK ST. CLAIR STOP AM SEND-ING ADDITIONAL TRAVEL FUNDS TOMORROW STOP WISHING YOU FAST RECOVERY STOP

Longarm showed the telegram to Lilly, who said, "You need at least a week to recover from that stab wound. You lost a lot of blood."

"I don't have a week to waste," he replied as he stretched out on his bed. "Besides, I'm not one to sit around. Lilly, I talked to Gloria, who was very close to your man Otto."

Lilly looked away. "I know of her."

"Well," Longarm continued, "Gloria was more to Otto than just another soiled dove. He actually wanted to marry Gloria and make an honest woman out of her."

"You mean he wanted to *marry* the woman?"

"That's right."

"Otto was very much a man who kept things to himself. Personally, I didn't care for him but Link thought he was reliable. Still, it seems hard for me to believe that Otto could have actually been in love."

"I believed Gloria," Longarm said. "I've been in this business long enough to be able to recognize someone who is telling the truth. That said, I'm sure that Gloria was telling me the truth about she and Otto planning to go away when they had enough money saved to start over someplace where no one knew of her sad and sordid past."

"Just you telling me this makes me think that Otto might have been a far more complicated and better man than I'd seen out at the ranch."

"There is something else of importance that Gloria told me."

"What?"

"She said that Link had once found gold in California."

"That's true. He talked about it incessantly when drinking. Link was one of the very few lucky ones."

"Also," Longarm added, "that he had hidden some gold in a town called Gold Hill."

"I heard him say that a time or two when he was really drunk," Lilly confessed. "But I always thought it was a complete fantasy."

"Why would you think that?"

"Link had delusions of grandeur. He believed he had nobility in his blood . . . kings and queens in England. And he would daydream about becoming a powerful politician starting as the governor of Colorado and then becoming a United States senator. He joked about one day becoming the president of the United States . . . only deep inside I sensed it was not at all a joke to him. He firmly believed that he had the looks and with his brief background as a federal marshal he would be able to get elected to high office."

"Is that why he became a federal marshal?" Longarm asked with surprise.

"It is," Lilly answered. "Link didn't give two hoots about catching criminals or upholding the law. He was callous, self-absorbed, and extremely ambitious."

"Do you think he robbed the train and also killed Otto and the Chinaman for their money?"

"I don't know," Lilly said. "But it's entirely possible."

"And if he took their money would he have used it to go to California and recover that lost cache of gold he hid near Gold Hill?"

Lilly shrugged her shoulders. "What you're asking is if I think that is where he is now and I honestly can't answer the question. Link was someone who would get all excited about something one day and completely forget about it the next. He was terribly addicted to opium and I do know that he would have had to have gotten a large and steady supply of it."

"I expect he did from your man Li Hop before he murdered him."

Lilly was quiet for several moments. "You know, I'm

starting to shake all over thinking that, if Link really did kill Li Hop and Otto Keisterman, then I am extremely fortunate to still be alive."

"I think that is a pretty accurate assessment," Longarm agreed. "But the real question I have to answer is where do I start looking for Link?"

"Anywhere." She reached out and squeezed his hand. "Custis, I'm sorry to say this but my husband could be anywhere by now."

Longarm smiled wryly. "Lilly, 'anywhere' is just too big a place. I have to either rent a horse and try to follow his trail through the Rockies or, if he went to Gold Hill in California, buy a train ticket and hope to find him in the Sierras just east of Sacramento."

"I see what you're saying," Lilly replied. "But I honestly can't give you any advice as to where he went."

"But if you *had* to pick a place, would it be Gold Hill in California?"

Lilly considered the question for a moment. "If you're certain that Link killed Li Hop and Otto, then he did it for opium and their money. But all of that together would not have satisfied my husband and he burns through money very fast. If he had cached gold in the Sierra foothills, then that is where he would go like a fox to its den."

Longarm nodded in agreement. "His trail from your ranch will have run cold. By the time I'm able to really ride the high country he could be hundreds of miles away. I think my best chance of catching him is to take the train to Sacramento."

"I want to go."

"No."

"Custis, I promised Nolita that I would help her get

back to Nevada and find out if her brothers are still alive."

Longarm could see the determination in her expression. "I can't stop you from doing that."

"But you *could* help me."

His eyebrows shot up in surprise. "Why should I do that? Nolita almost killed me."

"Can't you understand how badly she was treated and why she would just assume you were another horrible white man? She was terrified, Custis! You shouldn't take that attack personally."

"My shoulder took that butcher knife very personally."

"Just help me find her brothers and get her back to her Paiute people," Lilly pleaded. "If you will do that much, I will help you find my husband and forever put an end to all the questions about that train robbery and if the Dooley men were also involved. Wouldn't you want to have those questions settled in your mind?"

"I would," Longarm readily admitted. "Not that it would change the fact that I killed them in self-defense and they killed Charlie Oatman so all four of them deserved to die and rot in hell."

"Of course they do," Lilly said. "But for the sake of putting all of this to rest, I'm asking you to help me find Nolita's family and then allow me to go to Sacramento with you."

"Why is it so important you help me find him?"

"Because," Lilly said, "from the moment we met, Link was obsessed with me. And he still is in his own sick way. I don't want to spend the rest of my life wondering if or when he might suddenly appear filled with opium and lust and God only knows what else that has possession of his tormented mind. I want to once and for all either see him dead or hanged for all the murder and pain he has wrought upon me and everyone else unfortunate to have crossed his twisted path."

Longarm thought about what she said and he understood how she would feel. Who would want someone like Link St. Clair forever lurking in their past and who might appear at any time?

"All right," he agreed. "We have a deal."

Lilly smiled. "In that case I think we ought to sleep on it together."

"Sleep on it?"

"Or . . . whatever as soon as you are capable."

"Lilly," Longarm said, reaching for her hand and drawing her close to him on the bed, "I was born capable of doing that."

"I never had a doubt of it," she said, pulling away from him to undress.

Chapter 15

They drove out to the St. Clair Ranch one last time and
Lilly was silent, locked in her dark and troubled thoughts.
She closed up the place and their stay was brief, but
when she climbed back in their rented buggy to return
to Cheyenne, she remarked, "I had a little stash of my
own hidden money so we won't have to worry about
expenses."

"Billy Vail, my boss in Denver, sent me another one
hundred dollars and ordered me to find Link," Longarm
told her.

"Hang on to your money," Lilly advised. "I talked to
a man in Cheyenne about selling the ranch. I was surprised at how much he believes it is worth."

"So you won't come back?" Longarm asked.

"Never."

"No wonder that you bought a one-way ticket to Sacramento. Have you ever been there before or know anyone who lives there?"

"Not a soul, but I have enough money to get by for as long as it takes."

"So you mean you must have brought that expensive jewelry that Mr. Holt gave you in Denver."

"No, I sold it just before I came to see you in Cheyenne. I didn't know exactly where I'd end up but I wanted to have plenty of money so that I'd never have to be in anyone's debt."

"Between the money you had hidden at the ranch and the jewelry you sold in Denver, just how much money do you have?"

"Enough," Lilly said with a smile and then she would say no more.

Several days later they caught the westbound train out of Cheyenne with Nolita sitting in the seat before them, tense but also awed by her first experience riding the "Iron Horse," as she called it.

"Look at her," Lilly said one evening as the sun was setting across the Great Salt Lake Basin, "she looks like an excited little girl. I can't even imagine what she must be thinking as we get nearer and nearer to her Indian people."

It was true that Nolita had changed dramatically both physically and emotionally. Lilly had bought her new clothes, had her hair cut a little and combed until it shone like a raven's wing in the sunlight. The swelling in Nolita's face was almost gone and her eyes were no longer ringed with deep, dark bruises. Only a week earlier when she'd attacked him with that knife back in Wyoming, she had been desperate enough to kill and so beaten down that it had seemed unlikely she would ever smile again, much less laugh. But now, after a brief time in Cheyenne and on her way home to Nevada, Nolita was almost animated. She often cried out with glee and pointed to things that amazed her. The towns that they stopped at for water and coal for the steam engine were a complete visual delight and brought instant fascination. It seemed obvious to Longarm that Nolita had never been allowed to be seen in a town or city once the hunter and then the Dooley men had her in their evil grasp.

"Look!" Nolita cried, clapping her hands together and pointing to a passing town where cowboys were working a small herd of cattle in stock pens. "Cowboys! Big hats and good horses and they throw long ropes!"

Once, they passed a shepherd with a large flock of wooly-haired sheep. Nolita stared at them until they were out of sight and then she turned and said, "Sheep good to eat, wool warm in winter but stink when wet."

As their train rolled ever nearer to the high and empty deserts into northeastern Nevada, Nolita's mood grew somber and she turned very quiet. Her large brown eyes stayed glued to the window, and Longarm suspected that she was beginning to recognize an increasingly familiar land of sagebrush-filled long valleys and back-dropped by forever vistas.

"Do you recognize this country?" Lilly asked over and over. "Does this look like where you called home?"

In response, Nolita would nod her head, too overcome with powerful emotions to speak. At last, when Nolita saw the hazy Ruby Mountains, she once again became as animated as a child at Christmas.

"There! Over there!" she cried again and again,

loudly squealing, stomping her feet and clapping her hands with delight until other passengers turned around and glared at her with annoyance.

Lilly excused herself and moved a seat ahead to sit with Nolita and calm her down a bit. Longarm watched the two very different women with a smile pasted on his handsome face because he couldn't help but share the joy and excitement that the Paiute woman was feeling after being away so many hard years.

"Now," Lilly said, taking Nolita's hand as their train pulled into a small station about twenty miles east of Elko. "Before we get off and go to hunt your brothers, you must tell me again what you should say to them."

"I will say that I was taken by a white hunter who was very cruel to me and sold me to white men in Colorado to cook, cut firewood, and clean."

"And then what happened?"

"They were foolish men who tried to kill Marshal Custis Long but he killed them all first and then agreed to help find my family."

"That is right," Lilly said looking pleased. "You do *not* have to tell anyone what really happened to you all that time you were kept as a slave by the Dooley men. Only say that you kept their house, washed their clothes, cut their firewood, and cooked their meals. Understood?"

A tear came to Nolita's eye and it rolled down her brown cheeks. "But that is not *all* that I did!"

"The three of us know that but no one else needs to ever learn the whole truth."

"I hauled a lot of water, too. Very bad place. Stink much, you know."

"I know."

The place that they stopped and left the Union Pacific was a very small town with dusty streets, false-fronted businesses, and nothing much to recommend it from dozens of other hardscrabble train stops they'd passed since leaving Cheyenne.

"What's our first move?" Longarm asked the women.

"We'll rent a wagon and horses, then buy enough supplies for a week. I'll pay but you can do the dickering over prices. Men think that all women are easy marks and don't understand how to bargain."

"The last thing I'd call either of you women are 'easy marks,'" Longarm said.

"Even so, please do the bargaining and I'll do the paying."

"Sounds more'n fair to me," Longarm told her as he picked up their bags, and they headed down the potholed main street toward a livery whose sign was about four years late in getting fresh paint.

As they walked down the side of the street, staying close to the businesses to avoid being in the way of the occasional passing wagon, Longarm was well aware of the curiosity that they were creating. Men and a few women stopped and openly stared at the odd trio.

Most of the men sitting in front of stores smiled and even tipped their hats to Lilly, but none of them had so much as a smile for Nolita. Longarm had the distinct impression that it was not a common sight to see a Pai-ute woman walking side by side with a very attractive white woman.

"Why are they staring?" Lilly whispered.

"Not sure," Longarm replied, "but I don't think it's

because they want to be friendly and make our acquaintances."

"I have a *bad* feeling about this place," Lilly said. "Let's stay one night and be gone first thing in the morning."

"Sounds good," Longarm replied.

"Howdy," the huge liveryman said, stepping out to meet them in front of a barn that was more cracks than walls. "Nice day, huh?"

"We need a couple of horses and a buggy."

"Then you've come to the right place!"

"Looks to me like the *only* place," Longarm responded.

"How long do you need a rig?"

"Not sure," Longarm said.

The liveryman was not only tall but heavy and wearing bib overalls that looked to be dirty enough to stand all on their own.

"Let me put it another way then," the liveryman said contemptuously, turning his head to spit a stream of thick brown tobacco. "*Where* are you going?"

"Not sure of that, either."

The man spat again. "Mister, you don't look completely stupid but maybe you are."

Longarm grabbed the big man's nose between his right index and middle fingers and twisted it so hard everyone heard it crack. The liveryman squealed and tried to lash out with a fist but Longarm slammed a knee up into his privates and the squeal became a hoarse whoop, whoop born of agony.

Longarm could have broken the man's big hooked nose, but he relented and allowed the liveryman a few minutes to recover enough to blurt, "Only two dollars a day, mister, and you can drive the rig to hell and back for all I care!"

"Hitch us up a good team to a good wagon and we'll be back soon," Longarm snapped.

There were two poor-looking restaurants in a town they learned was named Dirt Gulch, and Lilly chose the one that had the fewest flies buzzing around inside. After they ordered, she said, "I told you that men bargain a lot harder than women."

"I guess I was a little rough on him, but he was arrogant and rude," Longarm said. "Two dollars a day for two horses and a wagon is reasonable enough."

"*More* than reasonable."

Nolita had not said a word since she'd watched Longarm bring the big liveryman almost to his knees. But now she looked over the table at him and smiled. "You plenty tough, Marshal."

"Tough enough," Longarm agreed. "Now let's order, eat, and get out of this place. Hope we don't get food poisoning."

An hour later and feeling their bowels rumbling with complaint, they finished up buying a few supplies and went to the only hotel in Dirt Gulch. "Need a couple of rooms," Longarm announced to the man who had been dozing behind a little table.

"I got some rooms, but not for any damned dirty-assed Indians," the man grunted.

Longarm glanced first at Nolita, who was studying her feet, and then at Lilly, whose face was turning dark with anger. He looked back to the hotel clerk and growled, "Mister, you need to change your mind in a hurry."

"About lettin' a squaw stay in one of our beds? Not even if she was whorin', which is what all of 'em do in this town."

Longarm was tired and out of sorts. He didn't like Dirt Gulch and so far he had not met one person that seemed even halfway friendly.

"Mister," he said, lowering his voice and bending over so he could speak directly to the man's face, "either you give us two rooms or I'm going to slap you from here to Denver and back, then I'm going to shove you headfirst down this hotel's shitter. Now, how does that strike you?"

He looked deep into Longarm's brown eyes and blurted, "Mister, you can have two rooms for two dollars."

"Sounds about right for this flea trap."

"My goodness," Lilly said after she had deposited Nolita in her own room and told her to lock her door for the night, "you really do know how to drive a bargain."

"Usually works out for me."

It was already getting late so they climbed into bed. "How's your shoulder feeling tonight?"

"It isn't my shoulder that you should be asking about."

She reached down and stroked his manhood. "Well, how's the big fella down there?"

"Ready, willing, and most of all . . . able."

Lilly stroked him until he was stiff and then she took him into her mouth until he was ready to bust. But before he did that, she impaled herself with his rod and then kissed his lips, tongue darting into and out of his mouth. Lifting her head she studied him with a smile. "Traveling with you is saving me money, Custis."

"I aim to please."

"How about *satisfy*?"

"I can do that, too," he promised as he began to thrust vigorously.

"I *like* traveling with you!" Lilly said, hugging him tight as her own pleasure mounted. "Any chance I can get you to marry me and we live on a nice little place in California?"

"You're already a married woman."

"I have a feeling that when you find Link that will suddenly change."

"Lilly, there's a part of you that is tough as nails and plenty nasty."

"Are you just figuring that out?"

Longarm grabbed her buttocks with both hands and went after her for everything he was worth.

"Lilly, how far do her people live from here?" Longarm asked the next the morning as they prepared to leave what didn't even deserve to be called a rail town.

"I asked Nolita that very question and she didn't know. Her people have wickiups, which I gather are brush shacks. They do have some horses, cattle, and sheep and they constantly move about hunting for game and good grass."

"So what you're saying is that we haven't a clue as to where to look for her brothers."

"That's right."

"Then," Longarm asked with no small amount of exasperation, "how are we ever supposed to find them?"

"Nolita says that when we get near her people they will find us."

"I just hope they recognize her and appreciate what we're trying to accomplish out here in this gone-to-hell country."

"She says that her brothers sure will."

"If they're alive."

"Yes," Lilly agreed. "If they're alive."

Longarm finished loading the wagon and helping the women up to the seat. "That liveryman sure didn't have much of a word to say to us a few minutes ago."

"That's because you almost twisted his nose so that his nostrils were pointing to the sky and probably left him with a pair of blue balls the size of cantaloupes."

"Yeah," Longarm admitted, "that probably had something to do with it."

They drove out of Dirt Gulch with the same bystanders giving them the same unfriendly looks that they had when they'd arrived.

"You know something, Lilly?"

"What?"

"I kind of look at towns like I look at most people."

"What does that mean, Custis?"

"I got this habit of sizin' them up fast and either likin' or dislikin' them right away."

"And you immediately didn't like Dirt Gulch."

"No," Longarm said, "actually it was *hate* at first sight."

Lilly linked her arm with his and used her other hand to give him a little punch in the ribs. "I like a man who makes up his mind in a hurry. What I don't like is a man who makes love in a hurry."

"Then you must like me plenty," he said, grinning.

"You guessed it. After we find Nolita's brothers and get back on the westbound, I'm going to start working on you in earnest."

"You're still a married woman, Lilly."

"Yes, and you're still a United States marshal trying to catch a train robber."

"My job is to try to arrest Link St. Clair and bring him to trial."

"Ha!" Lilly laughed out loud. "And I'd say that is about as likely as a snowball rolling straight through hell."

Longarm gave her a sideways glance and although she had laughed, there was nothing but dead seriousness written all over her lovely face.

Chapter 16

That night they made camp by a spring near the foothills of the Ruby Mountains. All day long, they'd seen signs of Indians and once even what was a small encampment in some rocks with four wickiups.

"Do these wickiups belong to your family?" Longarm asked.

Nolita shook her head. "Belong to all of my people."

Longarm lit a campfire while Lilly laid out some food that they had bought in Dirt Gulch. Nolita gathered firewood, far more than was needed for cooking but Longarm supposed it was to light up the night sky enough that it might draw her brothers or at least other friendly Paiutes.

"Nolita, have you camped here before?" Longarm asked after they ate and were sitting around the campfire getting sleepy and half mesmerized by the dancing flames.

"Many times," she answered, staring into the fire.

"How many more days do we need to travel before we stand a good chance of finding your brothers?"

Nolita shrugged. "Maybe tomorrow."

Longarm sure hoped so. He wanted to get back on the westbound train and get to Sacramento where he figured he had the best chance of finding or at least learning about Link St. Clair. Being out in this lonely country with two women who were counting on his protection was not to his liking. He knew that the Paiute had a history of trouble with whites and that they had often staged small attacks on the Central Pacific Railroad building crews some twenty years earlier.

"How many of your people remain in this country?" Lilly asked.

"Not many. Whites cut down the piñons whose nuts we gathered and used for our winter food. They shoot all the deer and wild things, put cattle on our lands, and kill many of our people." Nolita made a grand sweeping gesture. "Once, Paiute all over this land . . . but no more."

Longarm had been among the Paiute a time or two and he'd never been comfortable among them. They were short, dark people who lived in a country often so lacking in grass or water that it seemed impossible that anyone could survive. They were hunters and gatherers, not farmers like the Hopi and because of the scarcity of water and game, they were constantly on the move. Their traditional enemies were the Shoshone, but now it was the white man who came into this country seeking but rarely finding precious metals.

He heard the hoot of an owl and it was almost immediately answered by the howl of a coyote.

Nolita snapped out of her reverie and jumped to her feet.

"What is it?" Longarm asked, already pretty sure that he knew the answer.

"My people," she said, growing excited and moving away from the light of their campfire. Putting her hands to her mouth, Nolita twice echoed the calls of the owl and the coyote. All grew very quiet and the only sound was that of their horses shuffling their hooves in the dark and the crackling of their campfire.

"Nolita, are you sure that whoever is out there is friendly?" Longarm asked, taking Lilly's hand and moving out of the firelight.

Nolita stood frozen, straining to hear the faintest of sounds. Finally, she smiled and said, "Yes."

Longarm allowed himself to relax, but only a little. "Can you call them in to our camp?"

Nolita shook her head. "They will come with the rising sun."

Longarm nodded with understanding. "Lilly, I think we ought to try and catch some sleep."

"I'm not sure if I can."

"Me, neither," Longarm confessed.

"Nolita, what . . ."

But the Paiute woman was gone.

Longarm and Lilly slept poorly that night and they were wide-awake when the sun lifted off the eastern horizon. There were clouds in the sky and the sunrise began with a faint light that turned the sky pale gray and then progressed to salmon and finally the clouds became crimson and gold. It was as pretty a sunrise as Longarm had seen in many a day, but he was too tense to really enjoy it.

"One more cup of coffee," he said, more to himself than to Lilly. "Then I'm going to hitch up the team and we're heading back to Dirt Gulch."

"Custis, we can't just leave her out here!"

"It's her *home*," Longarm argued. "I'm sure that she's going to be fine. If she was worried about that, she would never have left our camp last night."

Lilly stared to the east, face troubled. "What if her brothers are both dead? What if her people decide that she is cursed or defiled?"

"I don't know the answers to those questions," Longarm admitted. "All I know is that we did our best to get her back to her people, and now that we've done just that it's time for us to go about our own business, and that starts with returning to Dirt Gulch and getting back on the train."

"Look!"

Longarm had been turning toward their camp when Lilly's sharp exclamation brought him back around. "Well, I'll be darned," he said as he saw Nolita walking toward them surrounded by about a dozen or more Paiute men, women, and children.

"What do we say or do?" Lilly whispered.

"We do nothing until they speak or make sign."

"But . . ."

"Shhh!" Longarm hissed. "Just smile and try to act relaxed."

Lilly edged up close against Longarm. "I sure hope that these are friendly Paiutes."

"If they weren't," Longarm decided, "they wouldn't have their women and children tagging along. And, most likely, they'd have attacked us in the night."

"I thought Indians never attacked at night."

"A lot of dead white men had the same wrong idea," Longarm said, smiling as the Paiutes grew nearer. Their men were armed with pistols and rifles and their women carried sharpened lances and knives. None of them were smiling and Longarm marveled at how strong and tough they all were.

"I have told them that you are my friends and are good," Nolita said.

"We appreciate that," Longarm said gravely. "Which ones of these are your brothers?"

Nolita nodded at two young men who stepped forward. "This is Samuel and that is Miguel."

At the sounds of their names, both young men nodded first toward Longarm and then toward Lilly.

"I am glad that they are alive and you have found your brothers," Longarm said. "Do they speak English like you?"

"No." Nolita spoke to them in her own tongue and then turned back to Longarm and Lilly. "They want me to say that they are very glad that you brought me home. They told me that they had caught the white man who took me away while he was sleeping and bashed in his head with rocks."

"He deserved that," Longarm said. "Anything else they want us to know?"

"Yes," Nolita said, looking uncomfortable, "they want also for me to say that they are all hungry."

Longarm killed a smile. "Tell them that there is plenty of food for everyone in the wagon and that they are welcome to cook it here."

Nolita translated this information and the Paiute women surged past her to the wagon where they and the children all began pulling out and then opening the supplies.

The Paiute men, however, did not move but continued to stare at Longarm and Lilly. Clearly, there was more unfinished business on their minds.

"What is it?" Longarm finally asked.

Nolita could not meet his gaze. "I'm very sorry but they want the wagon and horses."

Longarm was not completely caught off guard by this news. He had dealt with Indians before and knew that they usually felt that so much had been taken from them over the years that they were entitled to ask for almost everything except a white man's family or his weapons. Longarm chose his next words with care. "Tell them that they cannot have the wagon or the horses because, as you know, they do not belong to us."

Nolita passed this information to the men who began to talk about the manner with animated gestures. Nolita's brothers were calm, but several of the other men were clearly angered by this refusal.

Finally, Nolita said, "I am so sorry, but they will not leave you alone until they have at least one of the horses and all of the food."

"Is this how your people treat your friends?" Lilly demanded, clearly upset by what she considered to be ingratitude.

Nolita lifted her chin and met her gaze. "My people

have been hunted down by whites and while they believe me when I told them you are very good white people, they still see that you have much and they have almost nothing. Look at their clothes and at how thin they are."

Longarm felt a little ashamed because Nolita was right, these were very poor people. "If we give them one of the horses, then we'll have to leave the wagon here because it can't be pulled by the other horse all the way back to Dirt Gulch."

"They know that and the wagon will be useless to them," Nolita said. "But that is their demand. I am not their leader. I am a woman and cannot say what men will do."

Longarm turned and walked away to think about this for a few minutes. He was angered, but knew that no good would come from a serious confrontation that ultimately would go very hard on Nolita. The woman had suffered enough already and deserved better.

"All right," he agreed, turning back to Nolita. "Tell them to follow us and the wagon back to Dirt Gulch."

"They will not go to that place." Her brothers were speaking rapidly to her and when they were finished, she added, "They would be shot and maybe hanged in Dirt Gulch."

"Then tell them to follow us until we are close to that town and then they can have a horse and I'll have the liveryman come out to get his wagon. That way, Lilly and I are only in debt for one horse."

"I will tell them of this plan," Nolita promised.

Nolita conveyed Longarm's wishes and it was clear that some of the older men were still not pleased. But it seemed as if Nolita's brothers were openly in favor of Longarm's terms.

Longarm whispered to Lilly. "I think the best thing for us to do is to hitch up the wagon and leave at once."

"But . . ."

"Trust me on this," Longarm said as he began to grab harness and move toward the horses. "If we act as if we expect that they will accept my terms, then the likelihood is that they will. On the other hand if we look worried, afraid of them, or doubtful, they'll become even bolder in their demand for both horses."

"All right," she said. "I'll help you with the harness."

While the Paiutes argued passionately about what was to be done, Longarm and Lilly got the horses harnessed to the wagon and left their food supplies on the ground for the Paiutes to eat while they tried to come to an agreement.

"They're following!" Lilly said as they turned the wagon back toward Dirt Gulch. "The whole bunch including Nolita are hurrying after us on foot. Don't they have any horses?"

"I doubt it," Longarm said. "They are so thin that I imagine they eat their horses."

"Oh, my!"

"So before we get near Dirt Gulch you had better pick the one that is going to be butchered and roasted tonight," Longarm told her.

"But I like them both!"

"Think of those thin children following along," Longarm said, his tone of voice grim. "Think of how they'll feast for days on one of these horses."

"I'll try to keep that in mind," Lilly said, but she shook her head and her expression was one of sadness.

True to his word, Longarm drove to within a mile of Dirt Gulch, and in a deep and dry wash bed where they were hidden from sight of the town, he unhitched the oldest of their two horses and led it back to the Paiutes who kept glancing nervously over the edge of the river bank toward the nearby railroad town.

Nolita came forward and took the lead rope in her hands. "I thank you for everything you did for me," she said to Longarm and Lilly. "You will always be my friends."

"Here," Lilly said, slipping her a roll of greenbacks. "This is for you to help your people. Spend it wisely."

"I will," Nolita promised, hugging her tightly.

Longarm glanced over her head to the Paiutes who stood only twenty feet back. "Did your brothers accept your story about what you did while you were in the hands of white slavers?"

"Yes." Nolita allowed herself a small smile. "Forgive me, but I told them that *I* killed those Dooley men."

"You killed them?" Lilly asked. "And did you tell them how you could kill five bad men?"

"Yes. I was thinking about that all the time on the train coming to my land and people. I decided to tell them that I slit all the Dooley men's throats in the night while they slept."

"And they believed that?"

In reply, Nolita reached into her skirt and pulled out the same butcher knife that she'd used on Longarm's shoulder. It even had some bloodstains on the steel. "When they saw this knife they believed me."

Longarm saw humor and irony in Nolita's story. "You should have been a politician."

Nolita did not understand Longarm's meaning but she turned and waved the knife toward her people, who beamed with delight and appreciation.

Longarm pointed to the butcher knife. He made a slashing motion toward his neck with his stiffened hand. The Paiutes burst into gleeful laughter.

"Let's get out of here," Longarm whispered to Lilly, who was dumbfounded by the charade. "And the sooner the better."

Lilly touched Nolita's face and then she turned and hurried after Longarm and the horse that would live to see many more days.

The horse they had left behind cost them twenty dollars after some hard dickering with its former owner. He had tried to persuade Longarm that the animal was in the prime of its life while, in truth, it was a smooth-mouthed animal showing all the signs of advanced age.

"I would have paid him more," Lilly said as they climbed back on the train headed westward. "You didn't have to argue so hard about the price."

"That horse was twenty-five years old if it was a day," Longarm replied. "And he couldn't have sold it for twenty dollars to anyone. The truth is that he got more money from us than it was worth and he's probably telling all his friends that he slickered us good."

"I see." She paused a moment, then asked a question that she was afraid to learn the answer to. "Custis?"

"Yes."

"What will happen to Nolita?"

"What do you mean?"

"Will she wind up looking as bad as those other Paiute women we saw this morning?"

"I don't know," he answered. "She might. Then again, you gave her some money and she is smart. My guess is that she'll parcel that money out over a very long period of time to help not only herself and her family but the other members of her tribe."

"They looked destitute, didn't they."

Lilly was making a statement, not asking a question. Longarm scowled. "The Paiutes and all the other desert Indians have a tough go of it. Like we were told, once they relied on hunting deer and eating roasted pine nuts, which I've tried and are pretty tasty. But with all the white people tromping around on their lands, things have gotten a lot tougher."

"Will they as a people survive?"

"Yes," Longarm said without hesitation. "They will survive because that's all they do and what they do best. Some years they might lose more people than are born, but in good years they will replenish their numbers. They have one really great advantage over the Plains Indians like the Sioux, Cheyenne, Kiowa, and the Comanche."

"And what could that possibly be?"

Longarm pointed out the window. "The Paiute live in a mostly bone-dry and hellish country that has little or no value to whites unless gold or silver is one day found. You can't farm this land and you sure can't raise horses or cattle. This land won't even sustain flocks of sheep. There's little timber or anything else here so we've left it to these people who have lived here long before the pilgrims landed at Plymouth Rock."

"I see."

The train blasted its steam whistle and they began to roll. Weary and gritty, Longarm leaned his head back and closed his eyes.

"You're going to miss the scenery if you take a nap," Lilly warned.

"I've seen it all before many a time," Longarm answered. "And believe me, the country between here and Reno isn't fit for anything but jackrabbits and rattle-snakes."

Lilly was seated next to the window, and as they gathered speed and she studied the harsh landscape of sagebrush, rocks, and broken mesas, she nodded her head in agreement.

Chapter 17

Longarm and Lilly passed through Reno that night and then the train began the long, hard climb up a winding railroad bed that followed the Truckee River into the Sierras. Their pace was slow but steady, and it wasn't until the next morning that they finally topped the Sierras and began the descent into central California.

"I don't know how in the world they ever built a railroad over these high mountains," Lilly remarked as they enjoyed a leisurely breakfast in the dining car. "It seems impossible."

"That's what everyone thought when the idea was proposed for a transcontinental railroad," Longarm told her. "All the engineers said that it couldn't be done but Charles Crocker and his three partners, Leland Stanford, Collis Huntington, and Mark Hopkins, showed the world otherwise."

"With Chinese laborers," Lilly said. "Yes, I've heard that great story."

Longarm watched a four-point buck bound over a fallen pine to disappear into the thick forest. "The Central Pacific Railroad started out recruiting workers in San Francisco, but the men that came to the western slope of the Sierras to work proved to be lazy and unworthy. They were former miners, sailors, and the dregs of society and oftentimes drunks and derelicts down on their luck. Crocker and the Central Pacific would hire and transport them to the construction site east of Sacramento where they would work for a week or two and then quit or go on binges after their first payday. Finally, Crocker and his chief construction superintendent got the idea of hiring Chinese. The first ones worked out so well that they opened a big office in San Francisco and started sending ships all the way to China for more and more workers. The Chinese coolies came with the belief that they would build a railroad over these mountains, save their money, and return home to China as relatively rich men."

"Did they?"

"Some did but a lot of them stayed," Longarm told her. "Today, as we make our way down off this mountain I'll point out places where the Chinamen actually were lowered in reed baskets so that they could set dynamite and blow enough rock off the walls to build this winding roadbed for the rails we are passing over."

"My God," Lilly whispered, craning her neck to look down into a gorge that plunged hundreds of feet down to a raging river. "I can't even imagine how much courage it must have taken to build this high mountain railroad bed and then lay tracks. I'll bet the snows were a real obstacle."

"They were. Up here by Donner Pass the snows can get thirty or more feet deep. A lot of Chinese died in blizzards or accidents but still they kept coming from their homeland willing to take the risks to make what would be for them a fortune. Crocker's critics and detractors called the Chinese laborers 'Crocker's Pets,' but they proved to be sober, smart and hard workers."

"I don't know how they built that tunnel just under the summit that we passed through."

"That's a very interesting story," Longarm told her. "Want to hear a short version of it?"

"Of course."

"Well, the Central Pacific was pretty much stopped dead in a bad winter while trying to get over or through the summit. Given the snows and the elevation it was just insurmountable so they started tunneling from both the west and east slopes working to meet *under* the mountain. But they were using dynamite and it wasn't doing much damage against the hard granite. Even worse, after a charge blew, the workers would have to wait for hours so that the smoke cleared out of the tunnel. On some days, the Central Pacific construction crews counted their progress in feet . . . not yards. And then one day they heard about a huge explosion in San Francisco that leveled an entire city block."

"In San Francisco?" Lilly asked, making sure she had heard correctly.

"That's right. Some chemist there experimented with a liquid explosive and I'm not sure how he survived, but he did, and Crocker immediately sent for him and his explosive to use in the summit tunnel. Actually, they gave the chemist no choice but to come up to the summit where they built him a cabin away from anyone else and supplied him with all the chemicals he needed to reproduce the liquid explosive."

Lilly smiled. "And it worked?"

"Darn right it did! The man had created nitroglycerin and it was at least ten times more powerful than dynamite and didn't have the lingering smoke problem that kept workers from going back into the tunnel for hours on end. So this chemist began brewing his nitroglycerine and setting charges until at last the tunnel was completed under the summit. After that, the crews furiously laid track and the race on down to Reno and beyond to Promontory Point was in earnest."

"What a fascinating story! Whatever became of that chemist?"

"Damned if I know," Longarm answered. "Like so many others that have tamed the American West, he probably just faded into obscurity."

"But I'll bet that Crocker and the others that were building the rails westward made the chemist rich."

"I hope so," Longarm said. "Any man that would handle that unstable nitroglycerin deserved to be rewarded for his guts, brains, and daring."

"But the Irish built the Union Pacific out of Omaha," Lilly said.

"That's right," Longarm agreed, "and while the only high country they faced was at South Pass in Wyoming, they had plenty of their own challenges laying tracks. They faced blizzards on the Great Plains, wildfires that often stretched for miles and most of all they endured a constant threat of raids from the Plains Indians."

"How could those Indians have posed a really serious threat to so many men working on the railroad?"

Longarm had the answer. "The Plains Indians knew that when the Iron Horse cut through their lands, it would put a finish to their way of life. The buffalo would soon be shot out and indeed many were by passengers on the early trains. To stop the Iron Horse, the Indians attacked the small surveying parties and the forward bridge building crews. They knew they couldn't stop the big track-laying crews, but they sure played hell on the men that had to be way out in front setting up things for the actual track-laying crews."

"I see."

"You saw the sign where the Central Pacific and the Union Pacific met at Promontory Point. I would have given anything to have been there to witness the historic occasion back in May of 1869 but I missed it. I've seen pictures taken with the two train's cowcatchers nose to nose and hundreds of workers and dignitaries. But you know what is missing in all those pictures?"

"No, what?"

"Chinamen. Even though it would have proven impossible to build the railroad over the Sierras without them . . . they were and still are regarded with distrust and contempt by most Americans."

"Why?"

Longarm shrugged his broad shoulders. "The Chinese who came to America and stayed never really tried to fit in with the white society. They kept to themselves and still speak Chinese and retain their old customs and traditions. They have opium dens, dragon festivals, and are often very successful business people, but they do not mingle in the mainstream of our society."

"Why not?"

"Because of the prejudice against them and because that's just the way they want it," Longarm told her.

Lilly was quiet for a long time after that as they both enjoyed the magnificent views of the western slope of the Sierra Nevada mountains.

"What can I expect to see in Sacramento?"

"I haven't been there for several years, but it is a nice city to visit. It's located on the Sacramento River, which is big and a major navigation thoroughfare. In the days of the forty-niners, it carried a lot of men and supplies upriver from the seaport of San Francisco Bay."

"Wasn't Sutter's Fort there?"

"Still is, but Sutter lost his fortune when the hordes of gold miners swept over his land and stripped his fields, stole his livestock, and generally bankrupted the man."

Lilly saw a small collection of miners working a stream as they passed. "Is there still gold to be found in these rivers and streams?"

"I expect so but imagine that most of it has already been discovered and worked out. My guess is that there's still enough gold to keep a hardworking man in beans, but not much more."

"Those gold rush days must have been wild times."

"They were," Longarm agreed. "The forty-niner gold rush brought thousands of people out to the West seeking their fortunes. Most found only heartache and many died but it was still something that changed the course of our history. There have been other big gold rushes but none of more importance than the one that began at Sutters Mill in 1849."

Three hours later their train finally pulled into the depot at Sacramento. The town had grown considerably since Longarm had last visited, and from the freight that he saw being hauled on big wagons it appeared that the hide trade and agriculture were the main engines of this economy.

As soon as they disembarked, Longarm and Lilly took a buggy up into town and got a nice hotel room.

"What are we going to do first?" Lilly asked.

"Tomorrow we'll find out where this place is called Gold Hill and then we'll rent horses and strike out for it."

Lilly understood. "On one hand I want to find Link and put an end to him . . . but on the other I just wish that we could forget all about him and concentrate on seeing the sights and having some fun."

"I'm not here to have fun," Longarm reminded her. "I'm here on official business. Your husband probably instigated and planned that train robbery and there is little doubt that he murdered Otto Keisterman and Li Hop. I can't let him get away with that."

"I know." She tried to lighten her tone of voice. "All right, after we find and bring my husband to justice, what then? Will you stay with me for a while or will you go back to Denver?"

"I'll stay awhile," he said. "I've got a lot of vacation time coming and I've always wanted to spend a week or two in San Francisco and see Monterey."

"That's wonderful!" Lilly hugged his neck and kissed his face. "I'm so glad that you'll be staying with me to explore a bit. And who knows, maybe after two weeks here with me you won't be able to tear yourself away . . . ever."

"Lilly, please don't . . ."

She put a finger to his lips. "I know. I'm a married woman and you're a dedicated United States marshal who has no intention of being tied down by a woman."

"That's right."

"But people can change, Custis. People start out wanting one thing and then deciding they want something else entirely."

"I'm sure that's true."

"I mean to buy some land in California. I could use a partner."

"Lilly, could we talk about something else?"

She hid her disappointment well. "All right, what are we going to do first?"

"You mean like right now?"

"Yes."

He didn't have to think about that for long. "We'll get room service here and rest. Tonight we'll eat, sleep, and make love."

"I like that list but the order is backward."

Longarm locked their door and began to undress. "Then let's start out in that big poster bed."

Lilly undressed quickly and came into his arms. They both had not bathed since leaving Dirt Gulch and they were rank but neither of them cared as they toppled onto the bed and began to make love.

Chapter 18

"So Gold Hill is sixty miles a little to the southeast?" Longarm asked the Sacramento deputy.

"Give or take ten miles."

"Do you suppose there is a stagecoach that makes a run there?"

"Oh," the tall, laconic lawman drawled, "I'm sure that some of the supply wagons eventually wind up in Gold Hill but I couldn't tell you when. Most of 'em just take food and goods from here that have been unloaded on our river docks and then deliver them to the gold fields. They charge a fortune for doin' it and make a hefty profit."

"What do you know about Gold Hill?" Longarm asked.

"Not a single damned thing," the man said. "There are hundreds of little gold mining settlements scattered all over the western slope of the Sierras. Most of 'em at one time or another were boomtowns but when the gold was worked out they died. A lot of those towns aren't anything more'n just a few shacks and maybe a saloon or two."

"Sounds like I'd better rent a couple of horses."

"So you're not alone?" the deputy asked.

"No, I'm traveling with a woman."

The deputy grinned. "Is she pretty and willin'?"

"A gentleman never tells."

"Sure," the lawman said, smile dying. "My boss, the marshal of this town, is on vacation in San Francisco. He left me in charge and I suppose I ought to ask you why you are lookin' for a fella in Gold Hill."

Longarm sized up this man, who was his own height but considerably lighter. His clothes were dirty and soiled and he didn't seem real bright. "Well, I'll tell you, it is on official business."

"What'd he do?"

"Listen, Deputy, the man I'm after is probably living in or around Gold Hill rather than here in Sacramento. That being the case, I honestly don't see that it's any of your business."

The deputy blinked and his friendliness disappeared. "I don't much care for your attitude. You come here askin' me where the hell Gold Hill is and then when I tell you I get nothin' in return."

"I could have asked anyone on the street and gotten the same information," Longarm reminded the lawman. "But I will promise you this . . . if the man I'm after has come to Sacramento I will certainly let you and your boss in on that and tell you everything you need to know."

Somewhat mollified by this promise, the deputy relaxed. "See that you do. I've got business to attend to, Marshal. Expect we'll meet again."

"No doubt," Longarm replied as he headed up the street to find the nearest livery so that he could rent horses. Longarm had decided that sixty miles was too far for Lilly to ride in one day and a pretty rough distance for even two days in hard, mountainous country. But they'd do it, and his greatest fear was that Link St. Clair had come and gone with whatever gold he might have stashed in Gold Hill. If that was the case, they were looking at a cold trail again and Longarm just wasn't sure where he could pick it up.

He stopped by a telegraph office and sent his boss a short message telling him the situation and then Longarm found a livery and rented a pair of saddle horses.

"Be a dollar a day each paid in advance," the liveryman said. "Another fifty cents each a day for saddles and tack. Where are you and your partner headed?"

"Gold Hill and we won't be there for long."

"Gold Hill, huh?"

"Yeah."

The liveryman scowled. "I ain't heard much about that place in many a year. What kind of business you have in Gold Hill?"

"My own business. How far is it?"

"I think it's along the American River. Don't know for sure but I'd guess it's fifty miles to the southeast." The man's eyes narrowed suspiciously. "You ain't heard that there was another gold strike there after all these years, did you?"

"No."

"Then . . ."

Longarm decided that the people in Sacramento were about the nosiest folks he'd come across in years. "I'll be back to pay for two good horses in about an hour from now. Have 'em saddled and ready to go and they'd better be well shod. If I don't like the look of your animals, I'll go up the street and find a couple rent horses more to my liking. There are liveries all over town and I won't be cheated."

"Never occurred to me to cheat a man as big and tough lookin' as you, mister. I'll give you good, sound horses but I expect 'em back good and sound. Agreed?"

"Agreed."

Longarm returned to the hotel and collected Lilly. He told her what he'd learned and said, "We should buy a few provisions."

"Will we have to sleep on the ground overnight traveling between here and Gold Hill?"

"I doubt it," he said. "Most likely there are dozens of small mining towns between Sacramento and Gold Hill and I'll bet they are all hungry for business. I think we'll do fine. Probably take us two days of easy riding."

"And what if Link has already come there and gone?"

"I've been asking myself that very same question since we left Cheyenne," Longarm confessed. "But Gold Hill is the best lead that we have and so that's the one that we'll go after first. If Link has been there, I'm sure he will be remembered."

"Oh, yes," Lilly said. "Link is not someone that goes unnoticed."

Their ride to Gold Hill over the next two days was scenic and interesting. Longarm and Lilly saw plenty of men still dredging the rivers and streams and some were even using gold pans just like they'd done for thirty years or more.

"What happened to the face of that mountain!" Lilly exclaimed.

Longarm scowled at the size of the giant red scab blasted out of the forest and still leaking down into a gravel and mud field. "Hydraulic mining," he said tersely. "They used huge hydraulics with hoses to put tremendous force through nozzles that blasted away entire mountainsides."

"It looks awful."

"Yeah, it does," Longarm agreed. "And from what little I know, the runoff was so heavy with silt that when it carried downstream it turned bigger rivers brown, killed fish, and generally raised hell. My understanding is that they finally managed to outlaw the practice."

"I'm glad."

A few minutes later they came upon two ragged young men carrying gunnysacks. "Hey," one of them called out, "you wouldn't have a dollar or a little food to spare, would you?"

"That's up to the lady," Longarm said, glancing over at Lilly.

"Ma'am, we ain't eaten anything since yesterday morning and that wasn't but a little flour and water fried over a pan. We'd sure be grateful if you have something for us to eat or a dollar or two so that we can buy food next chance we get."

Lilly reached back into her saddlebags and found a couple of cans of tinned meat, a slab of cheese, and some crackers. "Here you go."

"Thank you kindly!" the taller of the pair said, giving her a slight bow.

"Here," Longarm added, tossing the pair two silver dollars. "Can you tell us how far it is to Gold Hill?"

"About ten miles right up this river and you'll come upon it. Not much there except a couple of stores that overcharge a man and a saloon with watered-down whiskey."

"Have you ever heard of a man named Link St. Clair?" Lilly asked.

"Sure have! He owns the saloon in Gold Hill." The ragged young prospector shook his head mournfully. "Is he a friend of yours, ma'am?"

"Quite the opposite."

The prospector brightened at this news. "In that case I can tell you that Link is about the meanest man you'll ever meet. He's the reason that Charlie here and I are so broke."

"What did he do?"

"He told us to eat up at the café next door and he'd pay our bill. Said he'd put us up for the night in his upstairs hotel room real cheap. But the next morning, St. Clair made us pay him ten damn dollars! Ten dollars is about three times what we should have paid, but Link has his friends there and it was made clear to us that we either pay up or get beat up. So we paid."

"How does he look?" Lilly asked.

Charlie shrugged. "I don't know. He's big and talks real loud. His eyes were funny-lookin' and we decided that he's takin' some drug. Maybe laudanum or . . ."

"Opium," Lilly said with certainty. "Link St. Clair favors opium and after that whiskey."

"Well, there is an opium den in Gold Hill. But we don't do that opium. We both get drunk on bad whiskey now and then but not that stuff the Chinese smoke."

"What's the name of St. Clair's saloon?" Longarm asked.

"The Dead Lilly," Charlie said, shaking his head in bewilderment. "Now ain't that one hell of an odd name for a *saloon*?"

Lilly's face suddenly lost its color.

"We'll be movin' on," Longarm told the two thin prospectors. "I hope you boys find some gold soon and get fattened up before winter."

"We won't spend another damned winter in this high country," Charlie vowed. "Too hard to make it in the snow and you can't work the streams and rivers anyway. Nope, me and Jed are headin' for San Francisco, where we mean to catch a freighter and work our way back around Cape Horn all the way to the harbor in Boston. We're done forever with California. We came out here together and we've been starvin' ever since."

"That's right," Jed said with obvious disgust. "We've both got achy joints from standing in icy water so long and our backs are shot so that we can't hardly stoop over and pick up anything without bones crackin' in our spines and knees. Charlie caught pneumonia twice and almost died both times. This is a hard, hard country and we're goin' home to see if the sweethearts we left to go and get rich out here are still available."

"They both probably gave us up for dead and got married by now," Charlie said sadly. "But if they did we'll get ourselves fattened up and slicked up and we'll find even prettier ones. Ain't that right, Jed?"

"Right as rain," his companion replied enthusiastically as the pair continued their walk out of the mountains.

"You were kind to give them two dollars," Lilly said as they rode along. "They sure looked used up for such young men."

"They did at that, but now we know what we have waiting for us in Gold Hill."

Lilly sighed. "I sure hate it that Link named his saloon the Dead Lilly. I wonder if that proves what I have thought all along . . . that he plans to hunt me down and kill me someday."

"Whether he does or doesn't is of no matter anymore," Longarm told her. "Because I'm going to either arrest him or kill him in the next few hours."

"He's real clever even if his brain is frazzled with opium," Lilly warned. "And he's snake-quick."

"So am I and my brain isn't frazzled."

"Can I ask you a question that has been bothering me?"

"Sure."

"Well," Lilly said, "since the Dooley men are *all* dead, how can you prove that Link was in on that train robbery?"

"Good question. Even though the robbers wore masks, I'm sure that someone would recognize Link and anyway that doesn't matter."

"What do you mean?"

"I'm going to get your husband to confess to killing Otto and Li Hop for their money."

"He'll *never* do that."

"He will if he wants to live long enough to go before a judge," Longarm quietly vowed.

Lilly glanced sideways at Longarm and saw the hard line of his jaw and the steely determination in his eyes. *Link is as good as dead already,* she told herself. *Because if Custis Long doesn't shoot him dead, I will.*

Chapter 19

They reined up their horses at a bend of the road, and before them lay the ruins of a forty-niner boomtown beside the roaring American River set down low in a deforested gorge. For several minutes, they just studied the derelict settlement with its falling-down buildings, false storefronts, shanties, and a big, abandoned ore-stamping mill. They could see the wooden bones of several big sluices that had been constructed to divert water to various claims and everywhere they looked they saw rusted metal . . . bed frames, piles of tin cans, bent and battered stovepipes, broken picks and shovels, and busted and rotting boards.

"At least they didn't blow away the side of the hill with hydraulic mining," Longarm commented. "That big, two-storied building in the center of Gold Hill must be his saloon."

"I never thought that Link would wind up in a place like this," Lilly said more to herself than to Longarm.

"He always was attracted to cities, lots of people and money."

"Maybe he's given up and this is where he decided to end up for keeps."

"I don't know," Lilly said as her face pinched with worry. "What are we going to do?"

"I want you to stay right here out of sight," Longarm told her. "Link has no idea who I am and that's my biggest advantage. If he sees us together, I lose that advantage completely."

"But . . ."

"Lilly," Longarm said sternly, "you promised to let me do this my way. I can concentrate a whole lot easier if I'm only worried about your husband and any friends that might be inclined to stand up for him in a showdown."

"But you don't even know what he looks like!"

"That's right, so why don't you describe him for me."

"Link is tall, but not as tall as you. I'd say he's about six foot two. He has thick black hair that he combs straight back, and he wears a handlebar mustache about like yours only it's black instead of brown."

"What else?"

"He . . . he has a scar that is plainly visible high on his right cheekbone. The last time I saw him he was thin, maybe weighing one hundred and seventy pounds. When you see him you will notice that he is very direct."

"What does that mean?"

"It means that Link seems to look *through* a person rather than just at them."

"All right, I get the picture."

"Oh, one other very important thing," Lilly said.

"Link is unusual in that he can do everything with both hands. He can write as well with his left hand as his right hand and . . ."

"Which side will he wear his gun?"

"This could have changed," Lilly said, "but Link didn't wear a holster and gun. He loves derringers and he could pull one out from his coat pocket, his sleeve, or his vest pockets. And he wears his pants inside his boots and keeps a knife in one of his boots."

"To stab or throw?"

"He can throw a knife and hit a playing card at fifteen feet every time unless he's drunk or drugged." She looked away, thinking hard. "I should also warn you that Link has amazingly fast hands with long, you would say almost delicate-looking fingers. And lastly, he has a very wide and disarming smile."

"Doesn't sound like I'll have any trouble picking him out from whoever else is in that saloon."

"No, you won't."

Longarm had dismounted to tighten his cinch and to settle his legs after the long hours of riding and to position his gun. Unlike many men, he wore his Colt revolver on his left hip, butt forward. He also kept a solid-brass twin-barrel derringer .44 attached to his watch chain. Many a time he had fooled someone into thinking he was checking the time of day only to surprise them with the nasty-looking and deadly derringer.

"Custis, I don't think I can stand to wait here not knowing what is going to happen to you in that ugly mining town."

"I'll be fine."

"You can't say that for certain!"

"Lilly, you have to trust me to do what I'm good at and just stay out of the way. I'll either arrest or kill him and it will all be over in the next thirty or forty minutes."

"But what if he kills you!"

"Then turn your horse around and ride for all you are worth back to Sacramento," Longarm told her. "When you get there, change your name and get on a stagecoach to someplace where Link would never think of finding you."

Lilly started to say more, but Longarm had heard plenty so he climbed on his horse and punched it in the ribs with the heels of his boots. He set off at a trot toward Gold Hill, wanting nothing more than to finish this job.

Chapter 20

As he rode into Gold Hill from the south, Longarm could see that the town was slightly more prosperous and populated than he'd first thought it to be from a distance. And although most of the early buildings were falling down, at least four or five new ones had sprouted along with a livery, blacksmith shop, dry-goods store, and a gun shop.

The Dead Lilly Saloon was the town's only saloon and there were four horses standing at its long hitching rail. Longarm dismounted and tied his horse, a compact bay gelding. He had a shotgun in his saddle boot and momentarily considered taking it inside the saloon but then he discarded the idea. A stranger entering a saloon with a shotgun would instantly attract unwanted attention and men would consider that a lethal threat.

Longarm unbuttoned his coat, straightened his flat-brimmed hat, and took a moment to scratch the jaw of his rented bay horse. "I'll be back," he said to the

animal, not really tying it but looping the reins over the
hitch rail so that, if everything inside went to hell and
he had to make a dash for his life, getting his horse moving would be far quicker and faster.

The interior of the Dead Lilly Saloon was nicer than
expected. The sawdust-covered floor was fresh and
untainted by years of tobacco juice being spit upon them
and the bar itself was long and polished with the grains
of its pine countertop neither scarred nor dull-looking.
There were a half-dozen card tables in the back of the
long, rectangular saloon, although only two tables had
players seated and they looked to be talking and drinking instead of playing cards.

The bartender was a thin, hatched-faced man with
deep pock marks in his pale skin. When he saw Longarm enter the saloon, he waved and offered a restrained
but cordial greeting.

"Welcome, stranger. What'll you be having?"

"A beer," Longarm decided, looking around and taking in everything.

"Be a nickel."

The beer didn't have a frothy head and it tasted
sour . . . and watery. That's what it was, mostly watery
and that reminded Longarm of what the two down-
on-their luck prospectors, Charlie, or maybe it was Jed,
had told him about the whiskey they'd been served in
the Dead Lilly.

"You stayin' the night or passin' on through?" the
bartender asked, trying to make the question sound
casual.

"Not sure yet."

"Come far?"

"Not too far."

"Where you headed?"

"Nowhere in particular."

The bartender was starting to look exasperated at the lack of information he was receiving. "We got some clean rooms with some pretty and willin' women in 'em. Might be you'd like to hold over here a day or two and have your pleasure. Café next door is first rate and reasonable although you don't strike me as a man down on his luck and out of money."

Longarm didn't offer a reply but turned toward the back of the room and the two tables of men sitting around drinking.

"You looking for a game?" the bartender asked.

"Maybe."

He pointed. "See that tall man in the bowler back there sitting with those two men wearing caps?"

"Yeah."

"He's the boss and he deals straight. If you are lookin' for a game, I expect that Mr. St. Clair might oblige you, although he generally don't play until later in the evening."

"Not sure that I'll stay that long."

"Look," the bartender said, "if you want to play a little poker or whatever, I'll ask Mr. St. Clair if he's interested in a game right now. I have to tell you that he don't waste his time playing for peanuts. If he plays, the stakes have to be high enough to interest him."

"Ask your boss if he wants to play," Longarm said, forcing a tight smile.

"Wait right here and I'll be back."

The thin, quick, and narrow-faced bartender hurried

over to Link St. Clair and bent low to speak in his ear.
Longarm saw Link turn and look him over and although
the distance between them was considerable, he felt
what Lilly had described . . . eyes that probed *through*
a man instead of at him. The other thing that struck
Longarm was how handsome, even in a state of dissipa-
tion, Link St. Clair still was.

The bartender scurried back to Longarm. "Mr. St.
Clair said that he might be interested in a game of stud
poker. Ante a dollar a game."

"Good," Longarm said with an indifferent shrug.
"Might be I'll do that after I finish my beer."

The bartender swallowed nervously. "Mr. St. Clair
doesn't like to be kept waiting on any man. Why don't
you take your beer over to the table and introduce yourself? Drink that one down and I'll bring you over a fresh
one on the house."

Longarm ignored the offer and launched himself off
the bar. He walked directly over to the table where Link
was seated with two other men. "So you're the boss
here."

"That's right." Link smiled, but it appeared to Longarm as if he had sneered. "And who might you be?"

"Just a man passing through."

"Without a name?"

"Name is Custis."

He looked at his friends with those dark, menacing
eyes and said loudly, "Ah, I believe that this Custis is a
quiet man. A person of real mystery!"

Longarm heard the soft, uneasy, and mocking laughter from everyone in the saloon. It made him think that

Link's companions feared, more than respected, him. And that could be to his advantage . . . or perhaps not.

"You play poker, don't you, Custis?"

"I play."

"Then pull up a chair!"

Longarm remained standing. "I've been in the saddle for a lot of hours and it kind of feels good right now to be on my feet."

Link frowned. "I can't play cards with a man who is standing."

"Maybe I'll play a little later."

Longarm turned his back on Link St. Clair and returned to the bar.

"Hey!" Link shouted, real menace rising shrill in his voice.

Longarm whirled, hand starting to move toward his gun, but froze when Link said, "You left your unfinished beer on our table. Not respectful at all, I'd say."

Longarm forced himself to relax and walk back to the table. He picked up the half-empty beer and returned to the bar. What he was hoping was that his behavior would be so unusual that Link's curiosity would get the better of him and that he'd feel compelled to leave his seated companions.

Which is exactly what happened.

"Who the hell are you?" Link asked, an edge in his voice as he bodied up close to Longarm and the bar. "I don't like people in my saloon who act . . . act unfriendly."

"I didn't think I was acting unfriendly."

"Well, you are," Link said. "What's your game, Custis?"

Longarm finished off the watery beer and set it down very deliberately. "I have something outside that will explain everything."

"Outside?"

"Right outside on my horse."

"Whatever you have . . . bring it in. You have gotten me real curious."

"Rather not bring it in," Longarm told him. "Kind of heavy."

"You look strong."

"Maybe," Longarm said, "but I'm also kinda lazy."

Link cocked his head, eyes studying Longarm as if he were an unusual insect or oddity. Longarm noticed the man was not wearing a sidearm, but he saw a bulge in Link's vest and figured it was a derringer.

"Mike," Link said to his bartender. "This man says he has something on his horse that we ought to see. Why don't you go get Stag and Shorty and let's all see what our man of mystery has to show us."

"Sure thing, Mr. St. Clair."

Longarm's mind began to race because the last thing he wanted or needed was for Link to bring a lot of backup protection. And it sure wouldn't take but a few moments for the man to realize that Longarm had nothing unusual tied across his saddle or hidden in his saddlebags.

The bartender called two hard-looking men from one of the back tables and when they were all together, Link smiled and said, "Lead the way, Custis the Mystery Man."

Longarm had no choice but to turn and walk out of the saloon. He moved slowly toward the bay gelding trying to figure out how best to improve his chances of staying alive now that the odds were so badly against him in a gunfight.

He stepped around the bay putting the horse between himself, Link, Mike, Stag, and Shorty. And in that moment, he yanked the shotgun from its boot, cocked back the hammer and threw it up over the saddle to level down on the dumfounded men.

"Freeze!"

Mike the bartender took off running like a spooked deer. The one named Stag dove behind a water trough. The man named Shorty started backpedaling as he clawed for his gun. Link St. Clair, however, shoved in tight against the bay gelding as his hand stabbed toward the knife in his boot top. The knife came up and Link drove it into the haunch of the bay horse, which screamed in pain and piled right over the top of Longarm, knocking the shotgun out of his hands. Longarm went sprawling as the bay fought to pull loose away from the hitch rail dally of its reins. Longarm rolled but not quite fast enough, and one of the horse's hooves slammed down on his thigh with the entire weight of the plunging, terrified bay.

Link hurled his knife across ten feet of chaos toward the scrambling Longarm and the knife missed by inches. Longarm rolled twice as bullets tracked his movement. He snatched up the shotgun and fired point-blank into Link, knocking him over backward with a huge hole in his chest. The second barrel disintegrated the horse watering trough, sending up a fountain of water and wood splinters . . . blood and bone, too, from Stag's shredded body.

Shorty was retreating and firing at Longarm, but he tripped over a fresh pile of horse turds. Longarm dragged his Colt out of his holster and shot the man in the face and neck.

And then, just when it seemed that it was over, two more men exploded from the Dead Lilly Saloon with their guns in their hands and caught Longarm off guard and completely vulnerable lying out on open ground. Longarm saw them take deliberate aim and figured he was going to die in this dirty street.

Suddenly, tightly spaced rifle shots exploded across the street and the two gunmen spun like tops, one collapsing on the boardwalk, the other falling and then crawling back into the saloon, leaving a thick stain of fresh blood.

Lilly was beside him before Longarm could even manage to struggle to his feet. "Lilly, keep firing at the door!"

She nodded and began to empty bullet after bullet through, over, and under the swinging bat-winged saloon doors. Longarm struggled to his feet, grabbed Lilly, and together they hobbled after the bay horse, finally chasing it down halfway up the street.

"Help me get in the saddle!" Longarm shouted. "I may have a busted leg!"

Lilly dropped her rifle and somehow helped boost Longarm onto the bay. He reached down, grabbed her wrist, and swung her up behind the cantle.

"Yahh!" he shouted at the bay as it plowed down the street running for all it was worth out of Gold Hill. "Yahh!"